Metaphorosis

July 2018

Beautifully made speculative fiction

Also from Metaphorosis Books

Reading 5X5: Readers' Edition
Reading 5X5: Writers' Edition

Best Vegan Science Fiction & Fantasy

Best Vegan SFF of 2017
Best Vegan SFF of 2016

Metaphorosis Magazine

Metaphorosis: Best of 2017
Metaphorosis: Best of 2016
Metaphorosis 2017: The Complete stories
Metaphorosis 2016: Nearly Complete Stories
Monthly issues

by B. Morris Allen

Susurrus
Allenthology: Volume I
Tocsin: and other stories
Start with Stones: collected stories
Metaphorosis: a collection of stories

Metaphorosis

July 2018

edited by
B. Morris Allen

Metaphorosis Books

Neskowin

ISSN: 2573-136X (online)
ISBN: 978-1-64076-112-4 (e-book)
ISBN: 978-1-64076-113-1 (paperback)

July 2018

Time's Arrow

C. Heidmann

In 2130 the Nelari began resurrecting the dead. In 2133 Talia's father called for the first time in five years.

"You want to bring her back, Dad?" *After all this time, after what you did?* Talia wanted to add, but didn't. Couldn't. Not to his face. Not anymore.

She barely recognized the white-haired, eighty-three-year old figure; the holo-projectors in her quarters relayed every etch-mark of time, his still-bright blue eyes peering at her out of a sagging, heavy face.

"Don't you?" He looked... hurt. Like when she was small and had uttered an expletive. How could she, his perfect little girl, have said such a thing? "But she's your *mother*."

"Have you thought this through? How it will be for her? For all of us?"

He rubbed at his left eye and blinked a couple of times. "You think I haven't? Ever since I got that notification, I can hardly think about anything else."

Talia's notification about the offer to reanimate her mother had arrived the previous day. Half-knowing it wasn't going to go away, she'd ignored it; until her father's call woke her in the middle of Copernicus Station's artificially maintained night.

"She deserves another chance, Talia."

Yes, but did he *deserve another chance with her?* She clamped down on the retort.

Twenty-three years earlier, Talia had lost her mother and learned of her father's infidelity in one afternoon. He'd been away on another 'business' trip which couldn't be put off even in the face of his wife's terminal cancer. When Talia tracked him down and gave him the news, he'd been heartbroken. The shameless display of grief had enraged her.

The pause lengthened as she concentrated on not fidgeting.

What could she say that would convince him she didn't want to talk? Not about bringing her mother back from the dead. Not about anything. She didn't want to get caught up again in the emotional turmoil of his dredged-up pain, his guilt, self-justification, or whatever new form his latest plea for absolution would take. It was part of the reason she lived off-Earth, as far away from home, from him, as she could get.

Her father's hologram fragmented as interference rippled it into multi-colored snowflakes, granting her a reprieve.

"Do you know how lucky we are?" he said as the holo-emitters recomposed his image. "If we'd not had her buried, if we'd had her cremated instead..."

"I know, Dad."

For their own mysterious reasons, the Nelari had revealed their technology in stages. Initially, only people who had been cryogenically preserved, a full body or a head, could be reanimated. Then the Nelari taught human scientists techniques for reviving the interred. Now families of the cremated lived in fervent hope that it might become possible to resurrect even those who had suffered complete body-loss.

"I thought you were opposed to the Nelari, Dad. You said you didn't trust them, that you don't believe in benevolent beings from the stars. Now you're ready to roll over and take their offer?"

He scratched his lip with his thumb. "I did say that. And I still don't trust them. There's no such thing as something for nothing." He shook a crooked forefinger. "One day those damned aliens are going to want something in return and payback's always a bitch."

She resisted the urge to roll her eyes. "They're not like that, Dad. In all their time here, they've not once demanded anything in return for their generosity."

"Then why don't you want me to take their offer?"

She rubbed at her rat's nest of hair. "I don't know if it's the right thing to do, I don't—"

"What do you mean not the right thing? Don't you want your mother back?" She didn't react to his accusation but the hardness in his eyes pushed at her, shoved like a playground bully.

"What about the rehabilitation? It will take weeks if not months, and you realize there's a chance she might not retain all her memory or personality when they revive her." Some reanimations had not gone well—people failing to re-integrate, like a graft not taking. Unable and unwilling to face life again, having never expected to be resurrected, they ended up in mental institutions or chose to end their lives again—with a stipulation to never be revived again.

A glint of moisture filmed her father's irises though he pretended it wasn't there. "I read all the literature. I know there's a chance we could lose her all over again."

"But you're not going to let that stop you, are you?" Certainty of his answer, his total conviction, sat like a lead brick in her stomach.

"You can't expect me to walk away."

"Why the hell not, Dad? It's what you did last time," she spat, instantly regretting it, suddenly tired and wanting to get this over with. She massaged the beginnings of a headache at her temples. "Why do you want my approval when you've already made up your mind?"

"Because that's what your mother would have wanted—us, united as a family."

"Since when did you care what she would have wanted?" The sound of her voice rising a few octaves spurred her on.

"You were the one who broke up our family. You walked out on her when she needed you the most." Ignoring the bounds of the holo-pickup fields, she gesticulated wildly, punctuating her words, slashing the air, decimating the millions of miles between them.

"I can't believe you're still holding on to that pain—"

Blood whooshed in her ears. "Her dying gave you an excellent way out of the mess you'd made of your marriage. You think she'd want to come back to that? To you?" She dreaded the return, hated the idea her mother would have to face it all again, her own tragic end, her husband's betrayal, the pain he'd caused her and the rifts it had opened in their family. Why couldn't he see that?

"Talia," he cast around him as if searching for his words, "listen to me. You don't know what it's like to lose a partner, a... a soul mate." His eyes tracked left to some point in the virtual distance, somewhere she could never see.

"Everyone who's lost someone wants them back, it's part of mourning. But we have to let them go, learn to live without them. Hasn't Mom suffered enough?"

She stepped back from the holo, folded her arms across her chest and became aware of her rapid breathing, accelerated heart rate. Finally, she'd run out of words, weapons to hurt him with.

This time his voice rose. "She *has* suffered enough, that's why I have to bring her back."

She had started it, but he wasn't going to let it go. She strove to keep her voice low. "Dad—"

"It's okay, I get it." He nodded as if he'd read her thoughts. "You don't want your mother back because you don't want *me* to have her back." He choked to a stop and lowered the accusatory finger he'd been brandishing. "You want to make me pay again." He was pointing his thumb at himself.

He was right. She wasn't denying her mother, she was denying *him*. But she clenched her mouth. Time had worn him down to a wrinkled, shrunken version of what he'd been, a badly made puppet of his former self. She'd said more than enough hurtful things to him over the years. This time had proven no exception.

In her father's world, a buzzer sounded. The evening mealtime call for the residents of Raintree Retirement

Village. His eyes flicked to his right, then avoided hers.

The buzzer sounded again. "You'll have to excuse me, I have to go." He rolled his chair away, an old man not wanting to miss his dinner.

"End connection," she told the com and headed for the medicine cabinet. She slipped a medi-film strip onto her tongue, let it melt into her palate. Within seconds, her headache disappeared, but the chagrin, the bitter aftertaste of their argument lingered. No instant medi-film remedy to soften that.

Did she really want her mother to remain dead just to punish him? She'd mourned, accepted the loss, and moved on. How could she go back on it now? How could her father expect her to retrace those painful steps?

Her mother had never yearned to be brought back to life and cured. And she couldn't be asked if she wanted to come back or to be left alone. But if obtaining consent was impossible, did that make it irrelevant?

Never before had it been necessary to deal with questions like these. When people died, that was it. End of story. Time's arrow had always pointed one way.

Death followed life, not the other way around. Until now. Until the Nelari.

In a few short months, she would have to face the reanimated version of her dead mother. What should she do? she wondered. What would she say to a mother she'd already buried?

"Hi Mom," was all she said.

The regenerated version of her mother smiled as she came into the waiting room. She looked incredible, radiant, and almost too beautiful. But her face didn't hide the shock, the disbelief, the pain and the disappointment when she saw how time had changed Talia and her father. She recovered and revealed nothing more as she greeted them in turn, asking the appropriate questions, keeping everything normal, calm, as if nothing untoward or overly emotional, were happening.

Talia had gone numb. When her mother hugged her, it didn't feel real. It was like holding a doll, an automaton. Who was this perfect imitation they'd been given? Why did she want to outright reject this manifestation of her mother? Why did she feel she had to keep her own emotional distance? Was it because she'd perceived this... this... ghost of her mother, as doing that?

She'd been coached, Talia told herself as she watched the apparition of her mother; prepared for weeks ahead on how to cope.

Her father was a mess. He began weeping the moment his past wife emerged. More than two decades of pain and guilt, and of mourning her, came out and pulped him, mashed him up like a losing boxer. He failed to stay up-right on his new Nelari-gifted cyber legs. They had to help him into a chair, get an aide to give him something to calm him.

Juxtaposed against Talia's decrepit father, her stunning, young 'mother' kept smiling, fussed over him in an over-caring, and to Talia, false way.

"Did you want to come back, Mom?"

All eyes in the room—including those of the bot-assistant who'd been facilitating the meeting, turned to Talia. No one moved.

"I... I, yes, of course, darling."

"Really? You wanted to come back?" Talia flung her forefinger towards her father, "to *him*?" Back in his mobility chair his tear-filled gaze pleaded with her.

"You remember how he hurt you? Abandoned you? Right when you needed him the most?"

"We can talk about this later, okay, Honey?" The manifestation of her mother tried to soothe. Was this her mother? Weren't they supposed to reconstruct enough of a person's personality to be indistinguishable from the original, assimilating every scrap of information left behind by, or about that person?

The resurrected woman's words seemed to de-immobilize everybody. Everyone started talking and moving at once. Talia barely heard them.

A timer display in her left vision flashed. "I have to go," she said in a loud voice. "My ship leaves in an hour. We talk now, or not at all."

They didn't talk then.

Outside, she blinked in the mid-afternoon sun, her space-accustomed eyes smarting in the harsh light. The trip to the spaceport was a blur. The whole way, she cried for her mother. Before her mother had passed away, she'd never spoken to Talia about what her father had done. She'd let Talia believe she'd accepted her impending death early on; that she'd been coping and that at the last, suffering and in pain, she'd wanted it to end, for herself and for all of them.

"Talia, wait."

It was her.

Almost through the departure gate, Talia paused. The reanimation of her mother stood alone, on the other side of the crowd, waving at her. Talia hesitated before weaving through passengers clamoring to get ahead of the line.

"I did want to come back," her mother started, out of breath, "despite everything. I... I mean, if I could have, you know, had a choice." Her cheeks were flushed, two distinct red patches on either side of her face, like Talia remembered.

Her mother had never been good with words, had had difficulty explaining herself. For the first time, Talia felt sympathy for her. Here was a woman scarcely her senior now, facing the prospect of going home with an eighty-year-old man, thrust back into a world she didn't know anymore. How would she pick up the pieces of a life death had made her leave so long ago?

"I'm... alive." Her mother's eyes shot full of tears. She shuddered in a breath and gulped. "I mean I'm glad I'm alive again. I can go travelling now like I always wanted to..." Her mother offered a smile. "I understand you live on a space station? I would love to see it, I mean, to see you... I mean, to talk... some time." Her mother hooked an imaginary strand of hair behind her ear. Despite her new short hair style, she repeated the action two or three times as if she still had the shoulder-length hair she'd lost to cancer and its medications so long ago.

The jittery little gesture triggered Talia's memories, countless instances when she'd seen her mother repeat exactly that nervous tick, always when her mother had been anxious, emotional. Talia's heart melted. It sounded like her mother, looked like her mother, *felt* like her mother. She grabbed her. "Oh, Mom." Her tears spilled unabated.

They hugged until the final boarding alert flashed red in Talia's vision.

Her mother went home with her father to the house bought back for her at great expense. Refurbished and re-decorated to as close as possible to the way it had been when she died. The pitiable, harmless-seeming gesture of a guilt-ridden erstwhile cheat and widower.

Talia wasn't surprised when they broke up.

It took about six months for everything to unravel before her mother found a younger man and moved away.

Talia's father died shortly after.

Her mother was still alive, of course, carrying on with her new life and her new beau. She might even outlive Talia now, might even be brought back from the dead again someday, like Talia would be.

But when the Nelari offer came to revive her father, Talia discovered that despite his insistence on resurrecting her mother, he'd neglected to specify his own wishes. He'd left the reanimation decision to his next-of-kin.

Her mother was hesitant.

"I... he said he didn't want to live without me. I... I feel bad... about the way I left him. But that house, the way he... I know all he was trying to do was atone, but I couldn't take it..." Another person hovered in the holo behind her mother, too far out of range to be rendered in detail.

"I felt like a ghost, like I was haunting him," The person in the background moved into the holo-frame and squeezed her mother's shoulder. She squeezed back. "What I mean to say is, I have Antonio now, and... maybe... your father deserves another chance at life too." She spread her hands, as if opening the best possible outcome.

At the resurrection and rehabilitation center, they let Talia in early.

She paused in the doorway to her father's room. He didn't notice her right away as two bots helped him upright out of bed. She eyed the figure of her dad.

Still eighty-three, still white-haired, he looked... invigorated, sprightly. Gone were the sunken haggardness, the slow movements, and the pallor that had washed him out. His cheeks had a rosy glow, almost like the cliché Santa Claus figure, and despite still being a little unsteady on his feet he had a quickness to his movements, a new sureness. Restored to the peak of health for his age, he should have another thirty, forty odd years of good quality life. More, probably, at the rate of Nelari-gifted medical advancement.

"You had me brought back." His soft words broke her reverie. Her mind had drifted. He took a step toward her, bots hovering either side in case he lost his balance. "Does that mean you've forgiven me?"

She opened her mouth. Had she? She bit her lip. She wasn't sure. But she was willing to try. In the post-Nelari world of selflessness and compassion, disallowing his resurrection would've been tantamount to purposely keeping him dead. She couldn't live with that; with herself.

If you liked C. Heidmann's story "Time's Arrow", leave a comment online at Metaphorosis. Authors love that!

About the story

A typical what-if moment inspired this story. What if aliens came along and made actual resurrection from the dead possible?

Aliens are, for me, the ultimate mystery and I strove to keep them mysterious in this story. If they are technologically advanced, they could be capable of anything—up to and including resurrecting our dead, and without necessarily explaining their motivations. —What if they truly were just benevolent beings from the stars, showering humanity with the benefits of their knowledge, sharing their technologies and advancements, without expecting anything in return? And who wouldn't want their dead loved ones returned to them? Who could say no to that? That last question brought forth the character of Talia and unraveling her motivations for maybe not being so keen on having her mother brought back from the dead.

A question for the author

Q: If your writing style were a bird, what type of bird would it be and why?

A: Nah, a bird doesn't work for me—unless maybe it could be a space-going bird! A bird is too limiting. It can only go as far as the atmosphere, around one tiny world, whereas I'd like to think my writing should be able to take me anywhere, out to the farthest reaches of the universe and beyond... into the multiverse, or whatever is outside our universe—and beyond even that.

About the author

Originally from South Africa, C Heidmann writes from Auckland, New Zealand.

Indistinguishable from a local after twelve years on the Outer Rim, she grew up on an entirely different galactic arm and relishes the idea of secretly being an alien.

@CarineHeidmann

The Forest of New People

Thom Connors

When winter comes to Vakning Forest, nothing changes. The evergreens, packed tightly together, don't wilt or become bare. Nor does the smell fade. As the winter deepens, the snow covers the canopy like a blanket, and the scent of pine needles and pine cones follows the only path worn out of the darkness.

Outside the forest, where the path begins, is the cottage of Abi and Odo Tremord. It has a red roof, brown walls, and a whitewashed, waist-high fence. In the yard stands a pine tree, a sapling, half as tall as the forest.

While the kitchen looks out over the pine tree, Odo's wood chopping block looks towards the forest. So it is that Odo is the first to notice any man exiting the forest.

It was always an adult, stumbling along the path on legs with newly formed muscles. The Tremords would take the man in, feed him, clothe him, and set him to bed. Then they'd teach him: wood chopping, speaking, etiquette. And when the season changed next, they'd see the colour on the horizon as the Bastler came trundling along, his wagon painted that garish orange. They would dress up the man in the finest clothes Abi had made, and all three would wait at the path's end for the Bastler to arrive.

When he did, the Bastler would get off the wagon. He would wave his black cloak around for show, with its purple inner trim and the wolf fur on the cuffs, and he would flash a smile which showed off his pointy canines, stark against the perfection of his other teeth. He would inspect the man.

"The forest made you mighty," the Bastler would say after checking the man's teeth with his eyes and a finger. Then he would push the man into the back of his wagon and get back in front of the horses, and prepare to leave. "Does he know when to run and when to walk? I can't set him to work if he can't show common sense."

"Yes, Sir." Odo would reply, every time. And then, "Sir Bastler, please."

And the Bastler would stop and look at the pine tree, the area around it always perfectly cared for by Abi and Odo, and he would look back into his wagon at the new man he had just been given, and he would say: "Look after the pine. Make it mightier, taller, until it can catch the snow."

"Please, Sir," Abi would say, gripping Odo's arm so tightly he would bruise. "Our daughter."

The Bastler would sigh and take the reins. "It's not enough yet to tip the scales. What is worth your daughter's life? This person? Any one person?"

Abi and Odo would slink back into the house and Odo would sink into a mood while Abi moved without feeling the things she did. And this was how it went, Odo chopping wood until he felt himself return to normal, and Abi preparing for the next new person to arrive.

At the end of the night, Abi and Odo would go out and clean and tend to the pine; rake the needles and cones out from beneath it, check it for rot and bugs, and measure it on the sunset shadow.

"It's getting taller," Odo would say.

And Abi would nod and force a smile, and wonder when she stopped believing him. Abi would glance towards the path to the forest and wonder what happened to the ones that went with the Bastler.

And so, that night, it was Abi who first noticed the person that stumbled out of the forest along a moonlit path.

It was a girl.

Abi covered her mouth with a hand.

"No, really. I honestly think it's taller now," Odo said, admiring their work.

Abi was shocked, too much to move. Odo watched her face and moved to hug her before he too noticed the teenager stumbling out of the forest.

Odo grabbed one of the blankets they piled by the door and ran out to meet her, draping the blanket over her and helping her into the house. Abi had moved into the kitchen and was working on dinner.

"Soup tonight?" Abi asked, her face blank. Odo could see the numbness painted on her face.

"I could eat," he replied. He walked the girl to the spare bedroom and laid her upon the bed. She didn't move, watching the wall. Occasionally her eyes would drift to the window that was just above the bed, as if she were watching the sunset.

"You're brand new," Odo said. "We're here to help you. Some of you can understand us and some of you cannot. But we are here to help, and if you have any questions, we will answer them. You get to be lazy for the next few days while your body learns to be, but then we will begin teaching you to be human; the appropriate times for laughter, when to run and when to walk.

"My wife is going to be very quiet when you meet her. She's going to have trouble with this," Odo smiled and used the end of the blanket to wipe some dirt off the girl's nose.

The girl reacted as a child, intrigued that something was reaching for her face. At no point did she flinch or move away. Odo did this every time, to teach them he was safe. Let them work for Abi's affection, for his he gave freely.

"Can you understand me?" Odo asked.

The girl looked him in the eye and Odo realised that her eyes were green, like the forest pines. And then the girl nodded and curled up in the blanket more tightly.

Odo slapped his knees slightly and then moved out into the kitchen. He shut the door quietly and walked over to the table where Abi had placed dinner, two bowls. Odo watched Abi's face and smiled when she caught his eyes.

"She's too tired to eat now. But she'll be hungry later," Odo said.

Abi sighed, picking up one of the bowls. "I don't want any."

"Then why would you...? Alright," Odo said.

"A part of me wishes to send you after the Bastler right now."

"We are not doing that, Abi."

"As soon as we can, she's going," Abi said.

"I meant that I won't go after the Bastler. We treat her the way we treated the men. Maybe this will tip the scale." There was a light in Odo's eyes that Abi hadn't seen in a long time. It filled the room a little, and made her believe, for just a second.

"We do it right this time," Abi said, glancing at the part of the pine illuminated out the kitchen window.

Odo reached over and grabbed Abi's other hand. He squeezed it tight.

"Will you come meet her with me?"

Odo didn't wait for an answer; he stood up and pulled his wife up with him until they were nearly hugging and then he guided her to the door.

"What did you name her?" Abi asked.

"I didn't name her. I want her to choose her own name," Odo said.

"Why?" Abi asked.

Odo opened the door. "I can't save her, but she can own herself this way."

"Can she?" Abi asked.

The door had opened on an empty bed, with a blanket thrown across it. The window above the bed was open.

"Did she run away?" Odo asked.

"Obviously," Abi said.

"None of them have ever done that before."

"Maybe she's different," Abi said, sarcastically.

Odo climbed on the bed and looked out the window. There was nothing, just the darkness past the light that shone out from the window.

"Do you think she went back into the forest?" Odo asked.

"None of the others have done that, Odo. I think she's still here, just around the house somewhere."

"Should we look for her?"

"No, let her freeze to death," Abi said.

Odo bit the inside of his lip and nodded. He didn't want to say it, but he could barely contain himself.

"Better she freezes to death than goes with the Bastler? Is that what you're thinking?" Abi said, with a loud scoff.

"I mean... Yes," Odo said, with a shiver. "But we need to find her."

"We do. Remember the time you tried to hide one from him?" Abi asked.

The Bastler had not believed them when they'd said there was no one. He had walked through the house silently. Then he'd raised his hands so that his thumbs entwined and his fingers made wings. He had aimed his hands through every door in the house until he stopped on the cupboard under the sink and their current trainee had crawled out voluntarily without the Bastler so much as saying a word.

The Bastler had left, just flashing them a forced smile. Abi had sworn that there was one extra tooth that was sharp in that smile. And after he had gone, the pine shed almost all its bark and they'd found black skinned insects they'd never seen before crawling on its skin for weeks.

"What did we call those insects?" Odo asked.

"Barkles," Abi said. She covered her mouth quickly with her eyes wide.

"Did you just giggle?"

"No. No!" Abi said. "I have no mirth."

Odo looked at her with loving disbelief but let it go. "We'll find her."

They searched the house for hours. Every nook and every cranny. They even lifted up the trapdoor to the basement.

"It took both of us to lift it," Abi said.

"What?" Odo asked. His fear of the basement reached his voice, so that he squeaked.

"How could this new girl with her brand new arms pull up the trapdoor when it took both of us?"

Odo breathed out so quickly he set off some dust, and began to cough. Abi pulled Odo from the entrance of the basement and let the trapdoor slam. As the trapdoor hit the ground, the room shook. And then, above them, they heard a shuffle.

Odo and Abi looked up together, at the roof that neither of them had even noticed for years. They rushed outside, Odo still coughing slightly. And there was the girl, her arms wrapped around the chimney so tightly that they were almost bloodless.

"Please come down," Odo said.

The girl shook her head.

"You could freeze," Abi said, flippantly, before whispering, "If she freezes up there we can just pretend we didn't see her, and then the Bastler won't blame us."

"If you let go, I'll catch you," Odo said.

Abi covered her mouth and her eyes widened again at this comment.

"You'll catch her? You?"

"Yes, I will. I am dexterous like a fox."

"You're stubborn, like a badger."

"You're the badger," Odo said, before turning back to the roof. "Please, just let go. I will catch you. And we will help you warm back up. There's a fire in the kitchen."

The girl looked at Odo and Abi. Abi finally turned away from Odo and looked at the girl, determined. "Let go," Abi said.

And the girl did, and she tumbled down the roof and Odo caught her comfortably. She wrapped her arms around Odo's neck and hugged him for warmth. Odo walked inside and laid her before the fire, and covered her in blankets. Then he sat in the chair before her and watched her. And Abi walked over and kissed his forehead.

"You were a good father," Abi said.

Odo said nothing, just leaned his head back on the chair. He let his head sit in the nook that he'd created over so many years.

"How long ago did he take Aroha?" Odo asked.

"I do not know if numbers exist that high," Abi said. "Since the sun could touch all sides of the forest at sunset. Since before the forest had an understory. Since the forest floor was clean. How long have the Apteryx been at war?"

Odo nodded and stared at the fire before placing another piece of wood on top. He watched the light spread, and saw how it bounced off the ceiling and threw shadows from the crossbeams.

"The Bastler didn't check the roof last time," Odo said.

Abi raised an eyebrow, and spoke. "No, he didn't."

"It's just an idea. And I only mention it because I didn't realise you were so sure Aroha wouldn't come back. I thought it was a game we played, that I said she would and you said she wouldn't, and we tempered each other to the middle that it was just a matter of time. But if you want this to end, I do too," Odo said.

"You made a promise for both of us, and I've accepted it. You keep wanting it to end. I just want us to be happy," Abi said, as she reached over to touch him.

Odo stood up to avoid her hand, picked up the girl, and carried her to her bed. When he returned he spoke quietly. "I'm going to bed."

Abi watched the flames, the way they reached out to her when she breathed in. And pushed back when she breathed out. Because in this place, at this time, she was the only thing affecting the air.

It had started when Aroha was three. Odo would wake up at midnight, sweat-glistened and scared, and run to Aroha's room and confirm she was okay. Sleeping, window open, with her sheets wrapped around her torso like a bandage. Odo would breathe again, fix the sheets over her and then walk back out into the kitchen.

He would check the newest forest man sleeping on the bedroll they'd laid out for him, warmed by the fire, and then crawl back into bed.

"Is there wood rot in your brain?" Abi whispered when he crawled back into bed. "She's fine."

"I know. I... What's happening to me?" Odo would ask, clinging to her for comfort.

"Your brain is noticing something. But only you are noticing it, Aroha and I are fine. So maybe you're just strange?" Abi muttered through her sleep haze.

Odo would laugh quickly and then press his chin into Abi's shoulder in a way that she loved, that made her wriggle against him.

"That's how we got Aroha; cut it out."

But Odo couldn't shake the feeling of danger that inched towards them. Odo would plan in his downtime, plan for the future, for teaching Aroha. For getting her a life away from the Bastler. Aroha wasn't part of the deal.

Odo woke the new girl the next morning, early. He showed her the clothes they had in the room still from their daughter. He dressed the girl and showed her how to tie her shoes.

"Can you speak?" he asked.

The girl tried and failed, her voice a croak.

"If you can climb a roof, you can start training."

She followed him out to the front yard and they began by sweeping the snow off the path to the door. The girl followed after Odo's actions. She learned quickly. Then they cleaned up around the pine, removing the needles and any cones that had fallen and setting them aside in a storage closet.

"Every day for the next few months, you and I will do these actions to get your arms and legs stronger. And then, afterwards, we will do exercise. And you will be able to outrun me, and out-jump me, and out-everything me. And then you will begin to chop wood with me and we will be ready," Odo smiled. And the girl followed Odo's actions and smiled back.

Odo realised that her smiling at him made him happy. So much so that he wasn't faking his own smile anymore.

"Also, when you are ready and able, you may pick your name. Whatever you wish. And we will call you that. Until then, think about the fact that a name is yours. It is the sound that people make to call you. If they can call you, they can get your attention. If they have your attention, they have your focus, and to have someone's focus is to hold magic in your hands. While you are here, you have mine. Just… mine."

She nodded.

"End of speech," Odo said and he began working through stretches and exercises he taught to all of the forest people. And as he did, he heard Abi begin moving around the kitchen making breakfast. They hadn't spoken since last night. They had fallen asleep facing away.

"We'll teach you sewing when you are able. Odo will make you strong and I will make you deft," Abi said as she placed lunch in front of the girl.

The girl nodded.

"You are going to hate this work. It will be very hard as your body learns how to make small movements rather than big ones. But it will become easier."

The girl opened her mouth and then closed it again.

"When you agree or want to show confirmation of understanding, you can say, 'Yes.'" Abi sat down beside her and picked up the spoon. Abi grabbed the girl's arm and put the spoon in the girl's hand.

Abi showed her how to leverage the spoon between her fingers and thumb webbing. How she should hold it still and move her mouth towards it so that any spills fell back into the bowl. The girl tasted the soup, left over from yesterday, and moved her head over the bowl, learning very quickly that it was the easiest way to get the food into her mouth.

The girl licked her lips and smiled very wide, tiny bits of soup dripping out the sides of her mouth.

"Yes," the girl said.

Abi laughed, and smiled, and then she nodded to herself. She reached up to pat the girl's hair. Then she stopped her hand and stared at it.

"Will you be okay without help?" Abi asked.

"Yes," the girl said, pride coming out along with more soup.

"Never speak with your mouth full," Abi said.

The girl closed her mouth and tried to say yes at the same time.

Abi became wooden as she stood and walked to the door. She walked to Odo, who was outside looking after the pine, raking its needles and the cones.

"Alright. What's your plan?"

Odo continued to clean as he spoke. He'd had the idea after the girl had climbed the roof. Then it had grown inside him and he didn't want to let it go.

"She stays up on the roof, and she can get the jump on him. Then we'll be able to kill him, and take his wagon and maybe... find her," Odo said.

Abi was quiet. She was studying his face, noticing lines on his face that she'd either forgotten or never really seen before.

"We'll need to tie her to the chimney, at the least hook her in with rope. Remember the bird sign?" Abi hooked her thumbs and held her hands out like wings. "The other guy came out of the closet on his own. And then there was the basement... What if she crawls off the roof?"

"That's a good point. What else?" Odo asked, shivering at his memory of the basement.

"Are we trying to kill him?" Abi asked.

"I am," Odo said.

Abi grew quiet, she walked over to the tree and leaned against it, feeling the bark scratch her back and trying to savour it.

"If we fail, he'll kill us."

"Feign ignorance. We had no idea she was up there or that she'd stolen the axe. How could we? No one came out of the forest since he was here last," he said.

Abi shook her head slightly and closed her eyes. "That's really weak. He'll see through it."

"No, he won't. Not if we believe it ourselves."

Abi opened her eyes and Odo was right in front of her. He kissed her softly, their lips touching for the first time in years. Their lips were both cracked yet, when touched, they sprang to life. They filled quickly, the pressure turning them red with blood and excitement.

Abi pushed him away slightly.

"Promise me you're not trying to get yourself killed," she said, the kiss still singing across her skin.

"I promise," he said, his lips pulsing along with his heart. He leaned in and held her. He rested his head on the pine tree behind her. There was resin in his eyebrow but he didn't care. He breathed her in, and she did the same, affecting the air together.

From the kitchen there was the clatter of a bowl.

Then the girl's head popped out of the kitchen window, right in front of them. A mess of black hair and smiles.

"Yes," she said, showing them her empty bowl. "Yes, yes, yes. More."

"Abi, dear," the Bastler had said after Aroha's fifth birthday. "Has Aroha begun to lose her teeth yet?"

Abi was tending the garden, not even looking up as the Bastler arrived. "Not yet, Sir Bastler."

The Bastler walked over and studied the tomatoes, potatoes. And the carrots, with their heads poking out the top of the earth. "You've done quite well to survive here. These are for the new people?"

"Some, sure. We keep the rest ourselves, for when I cook."

"Do you cook every meal?" The Bastler seemed incredulous.

"Of course," Abi said. "However dull monotony is, why wouldn't we cook?"

The Bastler gripped the crook of Abi's neck in a pinch as he laughed, loudly. "I'll be sure to bring you a cooking book next time. Maybe one from the Apteryx?"

Abi shrugged him off and stood up. She shouted into the house, "Odo. Hurry up." She cleaned her hands on her apron while affixing the Bastler with a look of contempt.

"You two really keep to your old ways, don't you? I'm sure Aroha is the proof of that. However, didn't you want a quiet life? A quiet, safe life? That's what Odo asked of me."

"Maybe Aroha doesn't want that?" Abi said as Odo emerged with a man so white he reflected the whole spectrum of the sun.

"Wow. The Apteryx have expanded, haven't they?" the Bastler said.

"We don't understand how it works, Sir Bastler," Odo said.

"Scales and balances, Odo. You press down on one side, and the other side changes. If the Apteryx make a tree, we get a person." The Bastler laughed.

"You know a lot about them, Sir," Abi said.

"I lived with them a time," the Bastler said.

Odo walked the man to the back of the wagon and then together, Odo and Abi walked the Bastler to the gate.

"As a favour, would you please save Aroha's teeth for me when they fall out?"

"That would make me uncomfortable, Sir Bastler," Odo said.

"I'll pay you," the Bastler said.

"With what?" Abi asked.

"Seeds. And cookbooks. Enough seeds for a season or one book per tooth."

"No, Sir Bastler," Odo said.

"I'll bring a book and some aubergine for next time. Aubergine," the Bastler said. He winked at Abi when he said aubergine.

"I love aubergine," Abi said, her mouth beginning to water at the thought.

Odo watched her face, and felt the fear rising in him again.

"No, Sir Bastler," Odo repeated, and he felt again the fear that kept waking him up at night.

"It's fine, I'll bring it with me next time anyway and we'll see what happens, shall we?" and then the Bastler left, as quickly as he had arrived.

"Odo, come see this," Abi said. She was grinning as he entered the room. Their kiss had sparked something faster than a fire. It was in the way they moved now, a string that tied them together.

Odo walked in the door and cleaned his hands, dirty and sweaty from cutting more wood. The fire roared day and night during winter, at Abi's request. Despite the relative warmth, she enjoyed the fire. And it gave Odo something to do, with all the wood they went through.

"Do it again," Abi said to the girl.

The girl licked her thumb, grabbed the end of a piece of thread and twisted it against her wet thumb. Then, tongue hanging out the side of her mouth, she threaded a needle and tied it off.

"Wow..." Odo said. "It's been ten days."

"Yes, it has," Abi said. "Damn, I'm good."

Odo leaned against the back of Abi's chair and his hand brushed against her back. Abi shivered when she felt it flash through her nerves like a wildfire.

"Yes," the girl said. She smiled widely and often.

"That smile could melt the snow. Be careful now, I enjoy winter, I want it to stay a little longer," Odo said.

"Cutting your wood all day," Abi said, grinning at the girl with a wink.

The girl put down the thread and sat like Abi, hands on her knees leaning forward.

"We have more sewing to do. What are you doing?" Abi asked.

"I have chosen a name," the girl said.

Abi and Odo slowly faced each other as Odo came back to the table and sat down as well.

"What name have you chosen?" Odo asked.

"Aroha," the girl said.

"No," Abi said, quickly. "You cannot have that name."

Odo reached out and grabbed Abi's hand and got no response. He took his hand back.

"That name means a lot to us. Choosing that name is impolite. It's like speaking with a mouth full," Odo said.

"It is important to me," the girl said. "I remember."

The girl who called herself Aroha spoke softly and forcefully, as if each word were chosen for more than one reason. She was learning so quickly that Abi and Odo were worried she would be speaking and understanding well enough to learn the plan before they told her.

"I remember," the girl said, "bark, resin, and bird song, there was yelling and calling for a word. It echoed off the branches, 'Aroha.' Only thing voice wanted in the world was Aroha. Being wanted is good. It stuck in the resin, 'Aroha.' It will be my name."

Abi didn't say anything, but Odo saw her sink into herself. She was remembering all the times they had both done that when Aroha had been taken. How many times had she and Odo walked through the forest calling, hoping that she would appear? As if the Bastler had just taught her hide and seek.

"When did you hear this?" Odo asked.

"I don't understand," Aroha said.

"How long ago?" Abi said.

Aroha shrugged.

"You have been with us for ten days. How many of this length of time was it before now?" Odo asked.

"Forever. Forever and then more," Aroha said.

"How long were you in the forest?" Odo asked.

Aroha tilted her head and looked at Odo. She stayed still, looking at him like an owl.

Abi wiped her eyes and smiled. "You want to be wanted."

"Yes," Aroha said, smiling widely and gripping the table.

"Then it is your name, and Aroha you shall be. And you are wanted." Abi turned to Odo. "Aroha can thread a needle, which means she's deft, and not once did she prick herself. You know what that means?"

"Axe time," Odo said, with a wide open mouth and fire in his eyes. Once he saw that Abi was smiling, he smiled too.

"Axe time?" Aroha asked.

"Axe time," he said.

"Come on," Odo said as he filled a bowl with water, and then dragged the newly-named Aroha outside. "You own yourself now. So I'm going to tell you a little something about me."

Odo walked out towards the wood block and picked up the axe he chopped the wood with, and the whetstone he used to keep it sharp. "There are two things that matter to keep yourself happy: someone who understands you, and a good whetstone."

Odo put the whetstone in the water bowl and then went over to the woodpile. He began rifling through the woodpile for anything that was useful, something easy but stable. Already split a little was best. When he found the perfect log, he took it back to the wood block and placed it so that the split was facing him.

Odo picked up the axe and sized it up, swung once and stopped short. He nodded to himself and knelt down beside the block and waved for Aroha to come over.

"All this wood has a grain. It's the easiest part to find. Some of it has cracks like this that are easier to split. We'll be aiming for this spot here. It's the mid-point between the crack and the edge, so once it breaks there, the rest will come apart easily. Aha," Odo said as he saw the whetstone.

"Once your whetstone has stopped releasing air, you take it out and you can sharpen your axe."

Odo took the whetstone and laid it upon his lap.

"When you sharpen an axe, it's not like a knife. You have to do it in circles. You place three fingers over the cheek of the blade and rest your palm on the beard, here. Then you take the bit, named so because it is the sharp bit, and you move it in a circle: toe, top of the bit, heel, bottom of the bit. You do this until you're happy with it, and then you flip it over and do the same again."

As Odo did it, he showed Aroha. Once he'd done one side, he handed it over and Aroha did the other. While Aroha worked on it, trying to get her circle right, Odo realised what his wife had done by sending her out with him.

"Aroha. We do these things because the axe is like a person, it can't always look after itself. Like you, when you arrived at our door, it needs training and help to be sharper and do its job. Do you understand?"

Aroha looked up from the axe and nodded, "Yes."

"When people you care about ask for your help, you need to do it. Sometimes it's not always clear. The axe won't tell you when it needs to be sharpened, but Abi and I will tell you. And we need your help. Will you help us?"

Aroha smiled and handed the axe to Odo, it was keen. As was Aroha.

"Yes. Yes, yes, yes."

"Even if it's scary?" Odo asked.

"What is scary?" Aroha asked.

And so Odo showed her how to hold the axe and cut the wood. And he thought of the Bastler splitting in half. And then quarters. And then eighths.

Aroha ran around the white-wash fence as fast as she could. Odo tried to keep up, and he did a respectable job. It took ten laps before Odo's pace was such that Aroha lapped him. She was laughing, her voice cutting through the silence and bouncing off the remnants of the snow.

Odo stopped and rested on the fence, watching the tree and looking into the kitchen to find Abi staring back at him. She smiled as Aroha lapped Odo again and slapped him on the back. Abi caught his eye and for a second they shared a genuine smile. Abi nodded inside. Lunch was ready.

"Enough, Aroha. It is lunch time." Odo walked towards the gate and held it open.

Aroha was still running, and ignored the gate. She vaulted the fence, using one hand as a guide. And then her foot caught on a post and her arm was pulled into a strange position. Her newly formed bones met the ground in a way they weren't prepared for and there was a sound, a branch cracking in a storm, and Aroha felt pain for the first time in her life.

Abi was out the front door faster than Odo could react. She was by Aroha's side, holding the arm.

"Can you see the bone?" Odo asked, quietly.

"No," Abi said, lifting Aroha to stand up. Aroha was crying now, replacing the laughter with something darker. The snow ate the sound and seemed to strengthen against its imminent melting. Abi spoke softly to Aroha, "We're going to splint this; it will be okay. The pain will pass, you don't have to cry unless it helps."

"What is cry?" Aroha asked.

"That is a wonderful question," Abi replied.

Odo shut the gate and opened the front door for them, his lips pursed.

"You should've been watching her," Abi said as they passed.

"This argument. Again?" Odo asked, trying to smile his way through it.

"Now? That joke is a good idea right now?" Abi asked.

"She will be okay. I'll grab some pine resin, find a splint."

"Hurry," Abi said.

When Odo returned with the resin and the splint, he found Abi bustling around Aroha and speaking to her calmly.

"Aroha, it's okay. You're going to be all right. There is nothing to be afraid of."

And the new person didn't cry or scream or yell.

She didn't move at all.

"You made a promise." Aroha had been nine, and the Bastler had been yelling. "As long as the Apteryx fight each other, you will be here. In this cottage. Bringing me the people that leave this forest. You will help me protect them and keep them safe. And now you wish to renege? You asked for the perfect life, and I gave it to you. And now you wish to change that?"

"Sir Bastler —" Odo started.

"No, quit it, Odo. You wanted a quiet life with your wife and I gave it to you. Why should we change that contract?"

"We do not want that life anymore."

"Because of Aroha?" the Bastler asked. He flung his arms around, his cloak trailing behind him. His rage quelled the forest around. It was spring, but there was silence. Despite the breeze, not even the pines moved.

Abi walked outside, drying her hands on her apron. Odo swallowed the fear in his throat and spoke firmly.

"We decided upon this together, you and I. We came to this agreement. But I no longer agree. We wish to take Aroha and leave. That is what we wish to trade," Odo said.

"Twenty teeth to break your promise? Are you insane? Or, do you think I am an idiot?' The Bastler asked. He walked towards Odo and through the gate without breaking eye contact. Odo stumbled backwards. The bottle he held contained all of Aroha's baby teeth. "More to the point, you lied to me. You hid the teeth, and you lied to me. You said they weren't falling out yet, and instead you'd been stockpiling them? To bargain with me?"

"I am sorry —"

"I don't care what you are, Odo. But the trees of this forest will know you as a coward." The Bastler spoke, and then called out to the house, "Aroha?"

"No. Just between us," Odo said.

"Did you try and bargain with him?" Abi asked, moving forward and shutting the door behind her.

"He did, Abi," the Bastler said.

"I said no. We spoke about this. We decided against it. How could you?" Abi asked. The hurt in her eyes wasn't fake, but it was quickly covered in fear. "Please, Sir Bastler."

"Bring me the girl," the Baster said to Odo.

"No, Sir Bastler. I'm sorry. Please, just take the bottle," Odo said, he held the teeth out but he was watching Abi, his heart breaking.

The Bastler knocked the bottle of teeth out of Odo's hand and it bounced on the grass. The Bastler walked up until Odo could feel the heat from his body. The Bastler, a full foot taller than Odo, leaned down on him. "People I cared about far more than you have made far more compelling arguments. And they didn't get their way either, Odo. Bring me the girl."

"Please, Sir Ba—" Abi started.

"Abi. He wishes to change the rules of this agreement. An agreement he and I have made. I wish to do the same. Bring me the girl."

"You have always been kind to us, Sir Bastler," Abi said, pleading.

The Bastler took a step back and scratched at his chin.

"You're right. Completely right. You have no reason to fear me," the Bastler said, as he licked his sharp canine teeth. "Aroha. Come here."

Aroha didn't come outside. She was nowhere to be seen.

"You didn't send her into the forest, did you?" the Bastler asked.

The Bastler made wings with his hands, his thumbs intertwined and his fingers spread outward. As he did, Abi saw one of his teeth sharpen, as his face twisted in what appeared to be pain. The Bastler shook himself off and began walking towards the house. Abi and Odo followed behind, slowly, unsure. The Bastler found nothing until he reached the trapdoor to the basement. There was a banging, as if someone inside were trying to get out.

The Bastler went over and lifted the trapdoor.

"Hello, Aroha. I haven't seen you in so long. You've grown big," he said. He held his hand out and Aroha grabbed it and climbed out. The Bastler lifted her up and held her against his side. "Did your parents put you in there?"

Aroha nodded and played with the cuff of the Bastler's coat, the wolf fur. "What colour is this?" she asked.

"It's purple. Have you ever seen that colour before?" he asked.

"No."

"Would you like to see a lot of it? I can take you on a trip and you'll be able to see a lot of it."

Aroha nodded. She was smiling at the shimmering cloak with its strange cuffs worn by the sharp-toothed man.

"That's not part of the agreement," Odo said.

"I want it to be," the Bastler said.

"No, please," Abi said.

"Aroha, go sit on my wagon, I'll be over in a minute," the Bastler said. "Say goodbye to your mother and father. You'll see them soon."

"Please, Bastler. We won't leave." Abi said.

The Bastler grabbed Odo by the back of the neck. "If twenty teeth is worth so much, how about you keep the bottle, and I take your daughter?"

Aroha hugged Abi tightly around the middle.

"Go wait by my wagon, Aroha," the Bastler smiled, pinching Odo's neck. "Tell her, Odo."

"Go wait by the wagon, honey," Odo said, his neck hurting too much for him to argue. He'd forgotten pain, it had been so long since he'd felt it.

Abi wouldn't let go, holding Aroha so tightly. The Bastler took Odo and dragged him to the trapdoor and threw him inside while Abi hugged Aroha's face against her apron, hiding the sight.

"Wait there," the Bastler said to Odo before turning to Abi. "Let her go."

"No," Abi said.

The Bastler walked up and grabbed her hand, pulling Aroha free. He grabbed Abi with his other hand, at the nape of her neck. He threw Abi into the basement and slammed the trapdoor shut. His face twisted in pain again. Then he picked up Aroha and carried her to the wagon, whistling through four sharp teeth.

"I'm calling it off. There is no way we're doing this now. None at all," Abi said.

"I know," Odo said. They were in their chairs. They'd splinted Aroha's arm and then put her to bed. She hadn't moved or spoken since they'd gotten her inside.

"She's not moving or crying at all. She doesn't want either of us in there?" Abi asked. She was so mad that it soaked her through. She could feel her clothes clinging to her with it.

"No, no reaction at all. Maybe she doesn't know how? Maybe it doesn't hurt her like that? Maybe they're not as normal as we thought," Odo rested his head in the worn nook. He stared at the ceiling. The roof beams that had given him an idea before now just danced to tease him. An idea that couldn't possibly be used.

"It's not happening. Stop trying to come up with another plan."

"I'm not." Odo sighed and rubbed his eyes.

"Because, I swear, Odo, I'm out. You made a damn promise about what our lives would be, and it was what we wanted, and now we run it to the end. Because that's what you're meant to do when you make a promise. I refuse. Look what happened when you tried to change your promise with the Bastler."

"I get it, Abi. I understand."

"Sure you do. That's why you keep coming up with these plans that get us hurt, or get Aroha taken. Instead of just completing the promise like a damned adult," Abi said. She was ramping up and Odo could feel it building in him like a tension, all the years of them making it work, all the hundreds of people that had come out of the forest. All of it making him want to snap.

There was a click behind them, a door opening. Aroha walked out, silent, her arm splinted and slung.

"What does this mean for the plan?" Aroha asked, softly. She looked at the floor.

"It means we're not going to do it, we're going to make you all better and then keep going," Odo said, walking over to her and checking her arm. He cupped her face in his hands and smiled at her, she didn't reciprocate.

"When you told me what you wanted to do, it was because the Bastler is bad. He is wood rot and wildfire. And we have to stop him. I want to help, still."

"No, Aroha," Abi said. "We're going to keep you safe."

"I don't want to be safe. I want to be good. I want to be an axe, the sharp bit," Aroha said, looking Odo in the eye as she spoke.

Odo smiled widely. "You can stay on the roof, and jump on him and then I'll kill him. Wood rot and wildfire." He chuckled.

"No. I said no," Abi stood up. "This is it. I've had enough of trying to change the rules. Why can you not just let this continue to happen the way you originally said?"

"How can you hide, when this idea can work? I couldn't have watched her. And look at how fast this new girl is learning, she'll try something soon, too. There is no option here. This isn't just a plan: it is the plan. You are barely alive. Live a little harder." Odo said, holding Aroha's good hand. Aroha wasn't smiling, her face was drawn.

Abi didn't move, just watched as Odo stood holding the hand of a girl that looked so much like both of them. What were the chances? Was it a sign?

"I feel pain," Aroha said.

"It's your arm, yes," Abi replied, still watching Odo.

"No, here," Aroha said. Dropping Odo's hand, she pressed at her chest, near her heart.

"Guilt," Odo said, trying to keep the smile out of his voice. "You feel guilt."

"Because I want to help, and I made everything worse."

"I know that feeling," Odo said. "A promise doesn't always mean what it seems, does it?"

Odo looked at Abi as he spoke, hoping the words would sink in, find purchase in a wife that he had started to thaw just like the weather outside. He hoped, breathed, and wished, that it would work. And then he remembered, and spoke. "Live a little harder."

Abi went to bed, but before she did, she nodded.

The Bastler's orange wagon arrived on the horizon with the sun a few weeks later. They'd removed Aroha's splint and moved her up to the roof as soon as they noticed the wagon in front of the sun. The Bastler arrived and disembarked, his coat with its purple inner lining seemed to shimmer and float behind him. He smiled and his sharpened top canine teeth seemed to threaten them.

Abi squeezed Odo's hand and whispered to herself, "Live a little harder."

"All this time and you two still hold hands? I am impressed. I had believed you both too... lost," the Bastler said.

Odo swallowed and squeezed back. "No one has left the forest since your last visit."

"Your arms are getting bigger," the Bastler said, walking over and squeezing Odo's left arm. "But your lies are just as bad as last time."

The Bastler pushed them aside and walked towards the cottage. Behind him, Odo and Abi stared at the chimney. Aroha wasn't well hidden, too tall for the chimney by far. But the Bastler's eyes were set on the door and he charged in, his hands out like last time, thumbs crossing with his fingers out like wings.

Abi and Odo moved to their spot, just outside the front door, so that the axe was within reach and the lip of the roof was where the Bastler would have to stop to speak to them. When they looked up, they saw her being pulled towards the Bastler whenever his hands aimed towards her. The rope tied between her and the chimney kept her in place.

And then the Bastler stormed out and stopped right in front of them. When he smiled his vicious smile, even more chilling now that his anger was oozing out, they saw that a third tooth was sharp.

"Where is he? I know there is one. Do you know what it costs me to keep spies among the Apteryx and to receive their missives? Sending letters across the world takes months. I shall not wait any longer. If you cannot provide the man, I will..."

The Bastler searched for words. While he searched, Aroha unhooked the rope and began moving silently towards him so that she could jump.

"If you cannot provide him, I will take... you instead." The Bastler pointed at Abi.

And then his arm slammed into the ground as Aroha landed on top of him. Odo grabbed the axe and swung it with both hands at the Bastler's head as Aroha scrambled away. The Bastler's eyes widened as he saw the axe moving towards his face. Abi couldn't watch, turning to hide.

Someone snapped their fingers, as if a twig had snapped underfoot, and the axe never landed. Abi, Odo, and Aroha were frozen, unable to move anything but their eyes.

"Ouch," the Bastler said as he stood up and shook his arm. "That was unexpected."

Then he looked and saw Aroha on her knees, trying to push herself to her feet with one arm, and he smiled. And Aroha noticed that three of his top front teeth were sharpened, as well as the canines. One for each person now frozen in place.

She tried to recoil at the way it made her skin crawl, but she could not move. The Bastler pulled her up until she was standing.

"A broken arm?" he said, looking at Aroha's arm. "I'm just... I'm so furious."

The Bastler unhid Abi's eyes and stood her up straight. He took the axe from Odo and did the same to him. Then he faced them towards Aroha. All three of them were staring wildly, the whites of their eyes showing just as much as their irises.

The Bastler reached up and opened Aroha's mouth and did the check he normally did on the new people.

Then he grabbed a tooth and pulled. The tooth came out smoothly, roots and all. A burst of air escaped from Aroha as the gum began to bleed and, for the first time in her life, she began to cry.

The Bastler sighed to himself and did the same thing to the first of his sharpened teeth. He yelled quickly before replacing the space in his teeth with Aroha's tooth. His bleeding stopped and he threw his sharpened tooth into the woodpile. He repeated it for all his sharpened teeth, even his canines. By the second tooth, Aroha began to choke as the blood filled her mouth, and the Bastler leaned her forward until the blood was rolling down her chin and pooling on the ground before her.

The Bastler yelled once more as he fitted the final tooth. He looked at Aroha's face after shaking himself slightly. He moved down so that she could look him in the eye.

"That was unpleasant, wasn't it? I wonder how many of you have ever cried before. Abi and Odo are wonderful; I bet you didn't even know what crying was when you hurt yourself. You are so new. You are the product of consequences. Of scales and balances, of the Apteryx making trees out of their enemies."

The Bastler took Aroha and carried her to the back of the wagon. He placed her inside, surrounding her in orange walls and locking the door before turning back to Odo and Abi.

After the Bastler had left with their daughter, the trapdoor wouldn't open. No matter how much they pushed, it wouldn't move.

"We need to get out soon," Abi said.

"I hope we die," Odo said.

Abi hit him, hard, in the shoulder.

"What was that for?" Odo asked.

"He's going to keep her safe, and we're going to get her back. Even if we have to beg."

"He said it himself, we don't dictate terms. We don't have a chance here."

Abi hit him again. "This is your fault. You were supposed to be watching her, and you were supposed to be saving her."

"I wasn't watching her. She was with you," Odo said.

"I don't mean physically watching her. You're a father, you're meant to keep her safe. Look what you did," Abi said.

"I tried."

"Well, you failed," Abi said.

They were in darkness. Their last candle had died three days ago.

"I swear," Abi said. "You need to stop this. We do things properly now, no more changing the rules. We're here until the war is over."

Odo nodded in the darkness.

"Promise me," Abi said, hitting her husband in the shoulder again.

"I promise," Odo said.

And then the trapdoor creaked, and clicked open. And Odo heaved and pushed it open so that they could both climb up. They could see quite clearly that the dust had literally settled since the Bastler had left. Their vegetable garden was in trouble, weeds and over-ripe fruit rotting. And there, in the middle of their yard was a sapling pine tree.

"Where did that come from?" Abi asked.

"I don't know..." Odo said. They stared at the tree, not touching, until the sun began to hit the horizon. Odo reached out to touch Abi's shoulder, and then let his hand drop. Then he went outside and began clearing up under the tree. "I can't find the bottle."

"What?" Abi asked.

"The teeth, Aroha's teeth. They're gone."

"I don't care," Abi said. "Tend the garden."

The Bastler stood before them and smiled. Though the smile was filled with Aroha's teeth, they fit perfectly in his mouth.

"I do not know what to do with you two. That's twice you've... Should I send bark-beetles after the pine tree again? Should I hurt your daughter?" The Bastler ran his tongue over his teeth, spending longer on his canines, as if he were wondering why they weren't sharp.

"The Apteryx taught me about consequences. They didn't intend to. It's their magic. I don't believe they themselves know how they do it. They talk about it as weight scales, with the tooth on one side and the person on the other. The cost of turning a man into a tree is your tooth. The scale balances. They're happy with that.

"It felt wrong to me, the idea never settled in my brain. Every time I tried to shut the door on it, it kicked up dust and swirled around. I couldn't shut the door on it until I knew. As it turns out, they were equating the wrong things. Cost and consequence aren't the same. Like with you. You promised to stay here because you wanted to be with your wife. The consequence is that you lost your daughter. But the cost? Your autonomy, your love, your happiness. All because one of the Apteryx took a liking to me and showed me a secret. Poor man, I haven't thought about him in a long time."

As the Bastler spoke, he arranged both Odo and Abi as if they were waving him goodbye. As he moved them, his breath, hot and warm, hit them on their necks and faces. It was fresh, and gummy, as if he had chewed pine resin. When he was happy with how they looked in their farewells he smiled and clapped his hands slightly. Then he got back into his wagon and snapped his fingers again.

Odo fell to his knees. Abi stayed standing, stoic. She didn't drop her hand, leaving it raised as if waving.

"Come now, traditions and all," The Bastler said. Holding the reins casually and staring out the corner of his eyes at Odo to prompt him.

"Sir Bastler, please. Return our daughter," Odo said, all hope and faith gone from his voice.

"No," the Bastler said. And he raised the reins.

"Please, Sir," Abi said. "Take me instead."

The Bastler stopped and his horses did, too.

"Repeat yourself," the Bastler said.

"I said, take me instead," Abi said. She hadn't moved, her hand still raised as if to wave goodbye.

"Why would I do that when I can punish you like this?" he smiled with two sharp canine teeth. There was no sound from Aroha in the wagon, still frozen.

"I can't do this anymore, please. Take me and return our daughter." Abi turned to Odo and lowered her hand to his shoulder. "He is a good father."

The Bastler watched and sucked on his new teeth.

"On one condition," the Bastler said.

"Anything," Abi and Odo said together.

"I don't want you, Abi," the Bastler said. "I want Odo."

"Yes, Sir," Odo said, standing up.

"No, Odo. Please, don't," Abi started but Odo quieted her with his hands on her shoulders.

"You two will be okay. You will have Aroha back, and you can get me back too.

It is a trade, I am not disappearing forever," Odo said. He didn't cry or fight.

"You promised me," Abi said.

Odo ignored her and turned to the Bastler.

"What do I need to do?" Odo asked.

"Go stand by the pine and raise your hands above your head," the Bastler said.

And so Odo did, and Abi tried to follow him.

"You stay here, Abi," the Bastler said, lifting up his hand to snap, as a threat. He got off the wagon, and walked over to Abi until they were staring eye to eye. He raised his hand until Abi could feel the wolf fur brushing her cheek, and while she stared into his eyes, the Bastler clicked his fingers. And then he stepped back and smiled, four sharp teeth smiling in Abi's face.

The Bastler got back onto his wagon and started the horses and Abi watched, afraid to turn around and look behind her.

"Please Sir Bastler. Aroha?" Abi called.

"Keep tending to the people. Until the Apteryx war is over. Then I will return them both."

"Their war with whom?" Abi asked.

"Everyone."

The Bastler left, whistling softly to himself.

The Bastler had noticed first. He had pointed at the tomatoes that Abi was holding.

"It will be a girl. Congratulations."

Odo was putting the forest's newest man into the back of the Bastler's orange wagon, with smiles and helping hands.

"I don't think they're boys or girls, Sir Bastler," Abi laughed.

The Bastler clicked his tongue in annoyance. His hands spread wide, his cloak showing its purple internal stitching behind him.

"My dear Abi, you are pregnant," he smiled, his pointed canines caressing his lips as they peeked out.

"Excuse me? How?" Odo asked as he shut the wagon door.

"Probably the same way it happens to everyone else," the Bastler said. He was holding back from clicking his tongue again. He did like these two; they were carefree and just happy. Happy with the trade.

"No, I mean, I didn't realise that was possible."

"Time hasn't stopped, my friends. You will still age, but as long as the forest keeps providing, you will keep breathing."

The Bastler had climbed onto his wagon and tipped a hat that had appeared out of nowhere, a pheasant feather stuffed into it.

"What will you name her?" The Bastler asked.

"We don't know, we'll have to talk about it," Abi said as Odo joined her, his hand around her waist. Odo was beside himself, hiding his excitement as best he could until the Bastler was gone. Abi was scared, but she didn't know why.

"The Apteryx have a word in their language: 'Aroha.' It means 'beloved.'" The Bastler dipped his hat and watched the couple hold each other.

"It's a pretty name," Odo said.

"It's a very pretty name," Abi said.

Two sharp teeth peeked out through the Bastler's lips as he smiled.

When summer comes to Vakning Forest it doesn't bring a heat wave. The air is humid but manageable and the animals that were silent for so long bring a quiet version of their music to the forest. As the summer extends itself, it grips the pine trees and pulls them towards the sun, ever higher over the path that leads out of the forest.

Outside the forest, where a path begins, is a cottage. Abi Tremord lives in this cottage. It has a red roof and brown walls, and a whitewashed fence. In the yard stand two pine trees. One is a sapling, the other is as tall as the forest.

If you liked Thom Connors story "The Forest of New People", leave a comment online at Metaphorosis. Authors love that!

About the story

Prior to being a musician, I was a Bastler. The story was autobiographical.

Seriously though, one of the things I love about short stories is that they allow you to explore things that may not have received the same attention you believe they deserved. Magical consequences are a big one. I loved the idea of magic that has consequences on the other side of the world and how that would look. I've been messing around with this idea for a while and could never figure out a way to make it work until I started to plan my move to the US. Doing so reminded me that I enjoy moving and a lot of people don't. As such this story focuses on people with different views on how happy they are with staying in one place.

A question for the author

Q: Do you make art other than prose? What kind, and how is it different?

A: In what now feels like another lifetime, I was a musician. I was that kid in school who wrote lyrics in class, and read when the teacher was speaking, and for most of my late teens and early twenties, I played shows regularly. In retrospect, it was the lyric writing that I enjoyed the most. That realisation is what pushed me into prose, then flash fiction, then short stories, and novels. While I still compose music and sing along to Taylor Swift in the car, I don't do shows anymore. But, I don't really know how to describe the difference between playing in front of a few hundred, or thousand, people and having a story come out. Can they be compared? In terms of writing them, songs are bursts of creativity and emotion. Stores require more planning, and definitely more time.

About the author

Thom Connors writes from his Macbook where the ' ' key is missing. This means that he refuses to use wors with the letter ' ', wherever possible. As such, talking of his love for 'ark fantasy tends to result in laughter.

Thom's longer works tend towards the fantasy fiction, while his shorter pieces are often general fiction.

The Dream Diary of Monk Anchin

Felicity Drake

I went to the museum's special exhibition on Seitokuji Temple alone, as was my habit. In the corner, there was a glass case full of portraits of the temple's famous poets.

The last portrait made me stop to take a second look. Unlike the other monks, this one was gazing directly out at the viewer. His face was painted in the standard Yamato-e style, just lines for the eyes and a hook for the nose, but there was something strangely expressive about the minimalist painting: a slight tension in the angle of his eyes, one hand holding a brush in midair, as if hesitating.

The bald little monk stared up at me out of his portrait, as if he were trying to speak to me. The plaque beneath the painting read:

Monk Anchin (1244-1316)
Collection of Seitokuji, 14th century,
artist unknown

There was no background or architectural detail in the plain portrait, but there was a lit candle-stand beside him, a common pictorial convention for depicting nighttime. Why would the artist take pains to portray Anchin, unlike the other poets, writing by candlelight?

Taking my notebook from my purse, I added Anchin's name to my notes on the exhibit. He couldn't have been a particularly notable poet. In high school, I had made a habit of memorizing poetry—which endeared me to my classical Japanese teacher and precisely nobody else—and even I had never heard of Anchin.

Before I left, I even spent 3,000 yen on the glossy exhibition catalogue, so I could take home a copy of the painting. My own research specialty is medieval Japanese women's diaries, and at this stage in my career, there isn't time to waste exploring intriguing tidbits outside my field. But seeing Anchin's little face, I couldn't resist the urge to find out what he had to say, what seemed to be on the tip of his tongue in his portrait.

It took some doing, but I tracked down a journal article about Anchin. The issue came out of the university's offsite storage facility crumbling and dusty. It was an obscure journal from the 1930s, with an article written by a professor I'd never heard of: "Annotated Selections from the Dream Diary of Monk Anchin."

I'll include an excerpt from the introduction here:

Monk Anchin's remarkable diaries are a treasure of the Kamakura period that have been overlooked for too long. Previous scholars have neglected his diaries, perhaps because of their length and the difficulties of his written style. Notably, in 1834 the scholar Ishizawa Takeru dismissed Anchin's diary as "an idiosyncratic work with minor poetic value and little historical interest."

It is regrettable that because of this early scholarly misinterpretation, no one has attempted a full transcription of the diary. Ishizawa reached his conclusion by reading the brief excerpt traditionally contained in 19th century anthologies, and I suspect that Anchin's dream diary has not been read from beginning to end in all the intervening centuries.

It is true that Anchin's diary is a singularly ahistorical text. He offers no information about daily life or special events at the temple; the diary reveals to us very little about the life of a monk at Seitokuji in the Kamakura period. Similarly, although his classical Chinese poetry was well-received by his contemporaries, subsequent generations considered his verses undistinguished.

But his diary is, nonetheless, a monumental and unique work: with fifty volumes representing the fifty years of his life after he took Buddhist vows, it is perhaps the world's longest continuous dream diary, full of insights into the unconscious mind of a highly literate, devout, and, yes, idiosyncratic man.

We can speculate about Anchin's life from court and temple records. Born the fifth son of a minor aristocrat, Anchin achieved some early success as a poet, but never received an official appointment at court. He never married, and took the tonsure in 1266, at the age of twenty-two. Although he spent the rest of his long life at Seitokuji, he was by no means disconnected from society; he contributed poems to social gatherings at the capital and frequently traveled on long pilgrimages.

I have selected the following excerpts from Monk Anchin's diary on the basis of their poetic or psychological significance. It is my hope that their publication will contribute to a reexamination of his life and work.

Since nothing had been written about Anchin in all the intervening decades, the professor's hopes had apparently gone unfulfilled.

Dreams were an unconventional choice of subject for a medieval diarist. But if he was best known for his dream diary, it explained why the anonymous artist had painted Anchin, brush in hand, beside a lit candle. As if he had just awoken from a dream and was hurrying to write it down. I've always been a vivid dreamer myself; when I was a teenager, I'd even kept a dream diary for a few years. I shredded it before I went to college, which I now regretted.

I settled down on my couch with a glass of wine and the diary excerpts. That was how I spent most of my nights alone at home, anyway, with Bach, Bordeaux, and books. And there was a certain transgressive pleasure in spending an evening away from my research or my students' papers, in the unfamiliar company of Monk Anchin.

First entry, undated but presumed to be from 1266:

Last night I saw a dream so strange I was compelled to take up my brush, to write it before it fled from memory. In my dream, a woman came to my bedchamber and sat beside my pillow.

"It's a shame when a good-looking man takes vows so young," she scolded me. "You've robbed the women of Kyoto. I'm terribly put out. At least we can meet in dreams, can't we?"

Her smile as she teased me was incomparably lovely. She outstretched her arms to me, and I saw that she wore her robe turned inside out—which once was thought to bring good dreams, as in Ono no Komachi's poems of longing.

When I reached for her, my hands passed through her body as if through mist, and she disappeared.

1267, the new year:
The first dream of the new year tells what is to come. A dream of a hawk is said to be auspicious, but what should I make of the dream I saw? Two hawks flew together through a clear sky. A cloud came and went, and there was only one hawk remaining.

1273, tenth month:
In last night's dream, I had retreated from the temple into solitude in a brushwood hut. There I would live in absolute simplicity, apart from the vulgar world.

A female pilgrim knocked at my door and asked for shelter from the rain. Although I should have turned her away (as the lady of Eguchi turned away the wandering monk Saigyō, so as not to tempt him), I allowed her inside and made her tea to warm her. We composed poems about the rain.

There is no escape from worldly desire, is there? Not in a temple, not in seclusion, and not even in one's own heart.

Anchin's dream reminded me of a dream I'd had as a teenager.

In my dream, I was waiting on a train platform. Rain fell down in a curtain from the overhang. I was in my school uniform, and my shoes and socks were soaking wet; a puddle grew on the concrete at my feet. The platform was deserted. Trains passed by without stopping, as if I were the only person left in the city.

A man joined me on the platform—an ordinary-looking salaryman in a gray suit, carrying a briefcase. He bought two cans of hot tea from the vending machine, and although all the benches on the platform were empty, he sat right next to me. But I wasn't afraid. We drank our canned tea together, as if we were the best of friends.

I was so young when I had the dream, I could hardly remember any more than that. It must have been written down in my old dream diary, but that was long gone. But I still remembered the thrill of it: to have the attention of a man, to be alone with a man, had seemed naughty and wonderful. It had felt so real. I remember waking up and hurrying to the mirror to see if my cheeks were red.

That had been just the silliness of a girl, of course. In my waking life, men had never paused to look at me, and I had never dared to speak to them. Since I'd started working at a women's college, it had become even easier to avoid men. I had been on a few dates, arranged for me by my worried parents or friends, but the silence had always stretched too long, and I'd never had a second date. There weren't many Monk Anchins left in the world, not many men interested in listening to a plain middle-aged woman talk about the fourteenth century, or in sharing a pot of tea and reading poetry together. 'Born in the wrong century,' my colleagues sometimes said about me, which I know they didn't intend to be cruel.

I brushed a few fragments of the journal's yellowing paper off my lap and set it aside for the night.

That Saturday afternoon, I sat at my usual table in the back corner of the department store's top-floor café, carefully arranging my papers and pens around the delicate china saucer and plate.

It was 900 yen for a thin slice of dark chocolate gateau and a cup of milk tea. Just a little luxury, something to sweeten the routine of grading papers. I hadn't made it to that coveted position of full-time professor at a proper university, where perhaps even grading papers would be a joy; at forty-one, I was still an adjunct lecturer at a two-year women's college, correcting grammatical errors and encouraging my pupils to look up information in books rather than on Wikipedia.

After an hour's work, I set aside the half-finished stack of papers and pulled out the rest of Monk Anchin's diary instead, savoring the bitter chocolate gateau as I read the last diary entry, written shortly before his death at the age of seventy-two.

1316, seventh month:
Now that I have been celibate for fifty years, all that was left of desire should have long since burned away, and yet...

I've seen the same woman in my dreams for years and years. I believe that I saw her once with my waking eyes. Not when I was a young man in the capital, and she a beautiful maiden, but when we were both withered and old.

It was at the height of cherry blossom season, when the temple was crowded with travelers. Through the crack of a door, I saw a little girl pretty and fresh as blooming dianthus, playing beside her grandmother. Unaware she was being observed, the woman didn't conceal her face; whatever beauty she'd had in her youth had long since faded, but her eyes were sharp, and her voice as low and sweet as a koto string as she read aloud to her granddaughter. And I knew it was her—not the greatest beauty, not the most charming or the most learned—but the same woman I'd seen in my dreams. I saw her in the waking world only this once, perhaps fifty years too late.

In my dream that night, she came to me, and she said, "When you were twenty, and I only seventeen, we both attended the Kamo festival. You stood beside my carriage then. I saw you, so dashing in your cap. I lifted my blinds in hope that you might catch a glimpse and slip a poem to me, but you turned your head left instead of right, and then you were gone. If you had turned your head right, do you think we would have known each other by daylight, not only in dreams?"

Last night, I saw her again. There were five-colored threads tied to her hands, which she offered to me to hold, like a bodhisattva welcoming me to the Pure Land.

"We'll part soon, even in dreams. I'll see you again," she said.

"Will we share a single lotus in the world to come?" I asked her.

"Do you think it's so easy to become a buddha? In seven hundred years, I'll make sure to come here once again. Promise me that you'll find me at Seitokuji. Promise me that you won't forget."

How appropriate that I saw her on Tanabata, a celebration of reunited lovers. Seven hundred years—whether Seitokuji still stands, or whether it is ashes, I'll be here once more.

In my career, I've read dozens of medieval diaries. I haven't found a publisher for my monograph yet, but still, I believe I'm something of an expert. Most medieval diaries, at least the ones that survive today, were intended for broader literary consumption, and therefore were thick with classical and poetic allusions, but Anchin's prose was unornamented and personal—almost uncomfortably so. It was unlike any medieval text I'd studied. I briefly wondered whether I should prepare a paper on the dream diary of Monk Anchin for a future meeting of the Medieval Diary Literature Research Group, but I couldn't imagine speaking about him in public. I wanted—strange as it was—to keep him for myself.

Monk Anchin died in 1316; thanks to his diary entry, I knew that he must have died shortly after Tanabata, the seventh day of the seventh month. It was a rather stunning coincidence that this summer happened to mark seven hundred years after his death, the year that he promised to return to Seitokuji to find his dream-bride.

I tried and failed to put it all out of my head. Over the next weeks, I read and reread Anchin's diary. I returned to the museum exhibit to sneak forbidden photographs of his portrait. And in my dreams, I saw: a pair of dark eyes, a crescent moon, a curl of smoke, half a line of poetry, dark woods stretching out beyond the cypress pillars of a temple's veranda.

One night, after the stimulation of Glenn Gould's magnificent Goldberg Variations and perhaps a too-generous pour of wine, I visited Seitokuji's official website. The temple still existed, and like some other temples struggling to pay the bills in an irreligious age, it offered overnight lodging for tourists. In addition to a gallery ' of inviting photographs showing off their austere guest quarters, contemplative gardens, and delicate vegetarian meals, there was an online reservation form.

According to the Gregorian calendar, Tanabata fell on July 7th, which was right before final exams and not a convenient time for me to disappear. But Anchin would have been using the old lunisolar calendar system, and the seventh day of the seventh month in the old calendar actually fell on Tuesday, August 9th (according, at least, to the online calculators I used). That was the summer holiday, and no one would notice if I left the city to go on a little pilgrimage.

With just a few cabernet-emboldened clicks, I had my temple reservations and train tickets booked. Perhaps it was silly of me, but I couldn't help but think that someone ought to be there to commemorate his life. Was I the only person alive who cared about Monk Anchin? No one had ever bothered to fully transcribe his diary. No academic had written an article about him since the 1930s. How sad to think that he had lived, died, and been utterly forgotten. What if he returned, after the promised seven centuries, and no one were there at Seitokuji to see it? I didn't want to let the date pass unwitnessed. That was all.

Monday evening, the night before Tanabata on the old calendar, I arrived at Seitokuji. I'd visited plenty of temples for research trips or sightseeing, to the point where all the intricately carved transoms and mossy rocks started to blur together, but this felt different. With every worn step I climbed, every statue I admired, I imagined that Anchin had stood in the same spot seven hundred years before. I'd never had a personal connection to a temple before. I had to remind myself that I still didn't have one: I was engaging in shallow literary tourism and self-indulgent fantasy, nothing more.

There were other guests staying at the temple as well. In the public bath, I sat across from a pair of little old ladies from Osaka chatting about the next stop on their vacation. In the corridor, I saw one of the temple's monks struggling to communicate in English and hand gestures with a family of Chinese tourists, and I wondered how they'd ended up at out-of-the-way Seitokuji. Seitokuji had a long enough history, but I'd assumed international tourists would be likelier to visit Kiyomizudera for its waterfall, or Ryōanji for its rock garden.

My room was spare and elegant, just bare mats, a futon, and a buckwheat-husk pillow. No television or wifi, which I appreciated; other than the slight buzz of the electric lights, I could imagine that I was back in the thirteenth century. A monk brought my dinner in on a tray: tiny bowls of tofu, vegetables, and rice, delicately flavored and artfully arranged. I wondered if Anchin had eaten so well here in his day, or if temple fare had been humbler then.

After dinner, I brought out my reading. Thanks to some archival wrangling, I'd gotten my hands on a copy of a facsimile edition of Anchin's diary. The copy quality was only so-so, and it was frequently indecipherable, but still it felt like a miracle to see Anchin's own handwriting. From the boldness or faintness of his brushstrokes, I could imagine the passages he had rushed to write, or the places he had hesitated, brush in hand.

After dark, I went out to the temple's veranda alone. Here, far from the city, I could hear cicadas singing and see the stars.

Anchin must have seen this same night sky, I thought, seven hundred years ago.

I sat on the edge of the veranda and stared up at the distant, unchanging stars. In my head, phrases from Anchin's poetry shattered and recombined. I felt so close to him here.

The faint scent of incense tickled my nose. No—cigarette smoke. My nose wrinkled and I had to pinch it to keep from sneezing. I glanced back over my shoulder and discovered the culprit: the teenage boy from the family of Chinese tourists I'd seen earlier that evening. He was leaning against one of the temple's cypress pillars, smoking a cigarette and staring off into space.

Well, the presence of an intruder, and one so rude as to smoke a cigarette in a nine-hundred-year-old temple, damaged my reverie. But I was hardly about to leave my perfect spot for stargazing. I'd been here first!

I tried to refocus. The smell of cigarettes was distracting.

I looked over again, and saw the boy stubbing out his cigarette and neatly disposing of the butt in a portable ashtray. Polite. I thought he might go back inside then, but no such luck—instead, he sat down cross-legged on the veranda, no more than a few meters away from me. He pulled out a little notebook from the pocket of his oversized jacket and hunched over it, pen in hand.

I took the time to look him over while he was staring down at the notebook. He couldn't have been much older than nineteen or twenty, and his gangly frame still had that elbows-and-knees pointiness of adolescence. His hair was long and shaggy, hiding some of his acne-scarred face.

Trying to retain some sense of solitude, I turned away and closed my eyes. I had come here to be with Anchin, to see if he had returned after the promised seven hundred years. Silly, yes, but...

My mind drifted, and among the cicadas' song, I heard another sound: the scratching of pen on paper. I glanced to the side, and there was the boy—biting his lower lip and writing away in his notebook. He looked utterly absorbed. My irritation at him ebbed slightly; in him, I saw a shadow of the bookish girl I had been when I was his age.

He looked up at me, and we were caught awkwardly staring at each other. I nodded politely at him—he stared at me, then hunched his shoulders and offered a tiny smile.

"No Japanese," he apologized, in heavily accented English.

"No Chinese," I answered, and I couldn't help but smile in return. I wondered why he and his family had come here.

I thought it might end there, but he stood, crossed the gap between us in just a few steps, and sat down again, right beside me.

"Can you read this?" he asked, again in English, and handed me his notebook.

He had been writing poetry—poetry in classical Chinese, at that! What a rare bird. Did they teach poetic composition in Chinese schools these days? My own students were about his age, and it was a struggle to get them to read even the most accessible poems, much less compose their own.

I took a moment to look over the poem. Clumsy in places, almost brilliant in others. A sudden pain ran through my chest. His handwriting was charming, neat and somehow masculine in the boldness of his penstrokes. And the poem wasn't bad at all.

"I can." For a few minutes I didn't return the notebook to him.

He handed the pen over to me, and I realized that he was hoping I would write a response. Ridiculous! As a medievalist, I'd read my share of poetry in classical Chinese, but I'd never written a single line of my own. Instead, I wrote out a quatrain that I remembered from Monk Anchin's diary. Anchin's poetry was in classical Chinese, so the boy could read it, and his style seemed to suit the atmosphere of the night.

I handed the notebook back to the boy, and he bent over it for a moment—then his head snapped up, and he stared at me open-mouthed. His brow tightened, and he said slowly, deliberately, "That is... very... good," as if it caused him physical pain to be unable to say more, to express what he was thinking. His English was almost as bad as mine.

"It is not mine," I admitted, because I could hardly take credit for Anchin's genius.

"Show me more?"

We wrote back and forth to each other. Some of his poems were his, some were famous verses that even I recognized. I replied to him with Anchin's poems, some half-remembered Li Bai, and a few poorly turned couplets of my own.

"My name." He wrote it out and pronounced it for me in Chinese; I had to repeat it several times before he nodded. I wrote my name and did the same for him. He looked so serious while he practiced saying my name.

The crescent moon had risen high above us while we wrote. I pointed to it, and he stared up at it with such earnestness, as if he'd never seen the night sky before. My throat hurt, my chest hurt. The stars reflected in his wide, dark eyes.

Suddenly, I was struck by the overpowering urge to tell him about Anchin. I hadn't mentioned Anchin or my unseemly obsession with a long-dead monk, not to anyone.

"Seven hundred years ago," I began. If only he had understood Japanese! It was a struggle to find the words in English. "There was a man. Here." I had forgotten how to say *monk* in English.

"At this temple?"

"Yes. He wrote this." I gestured to the poems I had written. "He saw dreams... every night, many dreams of a woman. He said he would return here—after seven hundred years—today—to meet her."

His forehead wrinkled in confusion, evidently unable to find the right word in English. He wrote a phrase in Chinese in the notebook, punctuated with a question mark. At first, I didn't recognize the simplified characters, but then I understood: *reincarnation?*

"Yes, that," I answered, pointing to the word in the notebook.

"Do you believe?" he asked.

"I don't know."

"I don't know also." His shoulders hunched forward and he stared down at the aged wood of the veranda: "I had a dream last year. I saw this temple, the moon, the... statue of Guanyin? Like tonight."

It was impossible, of course, but there were times one wanted to believe in the impossible. I had to acknowledge it: if Anchin had come back, it was in this boy's body. His great, dark eyes; his bold handwriting; his clumsy, potent poetry; his ungainly hands trembling in his lap as he tried to tell me about his dreams.

Why did he have to be a boy? Why did he have to be born in the wrong country? After seven hundred years waiting, couldn't we have been spared this?

"It's late. I should sleep," I said, because I didn't know the right words to say to him in English or in any language.

"Don't go."

A boy half my age, with acne-pitted cheeks and eyes as big and trusting as a golden retriever's... It would have been wrong to kiss him. I was old enough to be his mother. So I didn't—I didn't even touch his hand.

We sat together on the veranda without speaking, without touching, until the sun rose and the temple bells rang to wake the monks for the morning services.

It would have been rude to skip services after staying at the temple, so I dutifully attended, kneeling in the back of the hall. I hadn't slept a wink. The scent of incense, the dull gold gleam of the image of Kannon in the altar, and the monotonous chanting of the monks made my head spin.

I had met Anchin—had looked into his eyes and recognized him—and still the world continued to exist. The vulgar world, into which one or both of us had been reborn in the wrong time and place.

After services, the family of Chinese tourists said goodbye to the monks and hauled their bags down off the veranda.

I watched as if in a dream. The father swung open the trunk of the car and began loading up suitcases. The mother opened the passenger side door.

The boy tapped his mother on the shoulder, then ran back to the temple. He vaulted up the stairs to the veranda and stopped short, just a few feet shy of me. And then he stared, as if he were waiting for me to say something.

I tried to memorize his face. This was my last chance.

"Seven hundred years," I told him. "You will come again in seven hundred years. I will wait."

Would Seitokuji Temple still stand in the year 2716? Seven hundred years—I couldn't conceive of it. Even the few decades of solitude remaining in this lifetime were too much to bear.

He stared and stared, and then he shook his head. "I will study Japanese. When I graduate college... I will come here again. Two years. You will wait—you promise?"

I wanted to tell him that that was insane, that he was a young man with promise and a life and country and language of his own. That I was too old for him, old and strange and unbeautiful, not at all worth uprooting a life for. That I was willing to wait until the next lifetime, when perhaps we would be born in the same decade, the same country. That my delusions about Anchin were born of middle-aged loneliness and regret, that he was being swept up in teenage melodrama, that we both knew perfectly well *there is no such thing as reincarnation...*

But how could I say all that to him in English?

Instead, I said: "Two years, or seven hundred years. Either is okay. I will wait."

He reached out and touched the back of my hand with his fingertips. And then his mother called for him in Chinese, and he was gone, running off like a deer back to the car.

I watched him climb into the backseat of the car. The door closed. The car drove out of the parking lot and onto the winding road descending the mountain. It disappeared among the trees.

If you liked Felicity Drake's story "The Dream Diary of Monk Anchin", leave a comment online at Metaphorosis. Authors love that!

About the story

A few years ago, I went to see a special exhibition at the Idemitsu Museum in Tokyo, and I was particularly charmed by a portrait much like the one in the story.

Researching or translating premodern texts can feel like having a conversation with someone from the past, sometimes in a surprisingly intimate way. I wanted to write a story where that feeling of intimacy goes one step further, and to explore different ways people can connect (through reading, writing, dreams, language barriers, or reincarnation).

A question for the author

Q: Aliens. Are they out there?

A: In a vast universe, surely they are—although maybe in unfamiliar forms, or so far away that we can't meet them (yet!).

It's exciting to think that something so consequential is still totally unknown. It's good to have a little sense of mystery in life.

About the author

Felicity Drake is a writer based in New York. She writes fiction and interactive fiction.

www.felicitydrake.com, @DrakeFelicity

It Feels Like Déjà Vu

Phong Quan

I open my eyes and do the first thing I always do after running the gravitational field generator: remember my name. "My name is Jon, I'm a physicist," I say. Nothing comes after that. Thoughts begin to form and rise, and just as quickly sink back down; I feel like I'm struggling to stay afloat in a river that's slowly dragging me under, trapped in its constantly shifting currents. But I fight it. I know I have to fight it because... because that's what I always do.

"My name is Jon," I say again. The words are familiar and comforting and I grab onto them as if they can somehow pull me out of the river's rushing eddies and free of the haze I'm swimming in. I look around and see that I'm sitting on a bed in a room I don't recognize. I need to though, I need to... find out where... and when? Where and when... the generator shifted me? It's always... somewhere I have a connection to...

"I live in an apartment on Central Park West," I say, and my thoughts snap into focus and the river seems to suddenly stop, and then disappear.

Of course, this is my bedroom. I get off my bed and look around: my phone is unplugged on the nightstand, the screen still on and telling me it's seven in the morning; my clothes are thrown haphazardly over my desk, and as I walk past my dresser I see stacks of books with titles like "Buddhism A-Z" and "You are Here". Mom keeps sending them and I keep promising but never having the time to read them.

I walk out of the bedroom and into a living room as messy and chaotic as my life must be even in this reality: empty take-out boxes cover my small dinner table, dozens of unopened packages from Amazon litter the floor, and piles of mail lean against stacks of paper. Next to my

TV, and covered with the same fine layer of dust, the hand-carved wooden Buddha Mom gave me for my birthday sits silently contemplating the disorder. I really haven't been a good son.

But everything seems right so far, though I know that doesn't mean anything until I get to the lab and run the calculations. I smile anyway, glad to feel some memories I'm sure are real coming back. I make my way through the mess of my living room to the large windows and look outside. Across the street I see the red-orange leaves of the trees that mark the edge of Central Park.

My smile slips. This isn't right. This was a big shift—a change this large hasn't happened in a while.

I feel the memory come to me then the same way they always do: washing over me in a tingling wave of déjà vu. I remember standing here, looking across the street at the bright green leaves of the trees that mark the edge of Central Park. Then and now, I turn and see something I hadn't noticed before.

"It's a lotus flower," she says. "It should bloom by the end of summer if you manage not to kill it first. I think even you'll be okay with this one though—it's super easy to

take care of. You just need to keep the water level right, and then just let it grow." *She gently brushes her fingers across the bulb of the flower before drawing her hand away.*

The memory fades and I see the flower in the smooth white bowl by the window: a bright red teardrop on the face of a gray winter sky. Its familiarity tugs at me, but I know I've never seen it before. I've always been bad with plants—I even managed to kill my parents' lawn once by over-watering it.

I push it aside. It's a minor change and as long as I'm careful to keep my real memories separate from the fake ones from this shift, I'll be okay. Or at least I won't get any worse.

But I know that while this may be my apartment, I'm not *home*. I know that because the trees in Central Park are still standing and New York isn't flooded.

I call a car to take me to the lab at 50 Hudson Yards, where the generator always is. For some reason it's always there. The gravitational fields it generates are strong enough to warp space-time to such an extent that it can send me into another life and reality, but it never moves itself.

It'd probably be faster to take the train, but I want to keep a door between me and the city's rush hour madness. The time right after a test is the most dangerous. Anything—the faintest smell, the most innocuous sound—could trigger a flash of déjà vu and I would lose a bit more of my real self—of home—buried under the memories of lives I never lived.

So as the car takes me downtown and past the signs of damage that must have been from Superstorm Tammy—shuttered stores, missing trees and power lines, and construction around a damaged Javits Center that tells me I must be at least a few months removed from the storm this time—I imagine it even worse, I remember it even worse. I see rain pouring down in endless sheets between the steel and glass buildings. Trees and signs bend and creak and I feel water soaking into me as I slowly push against the howling wind. I hear an angry roar and look up to see water rushing down the street, swallowing up cars and people, their mouths open in screams I can't hear over the storm.

Thunder fills my ears, my heart jumps into my throat, and the car stops.

"You have arrived at 50 Hudson Yards," it tells me.

I've been the only one in the main lab on the 40th floor for hours now, alone with rows of messy tables and computers. I'm in front of a digital board, scrawling down the last set of my equations. These are the equations that, once completed with data from this reality's generator to determine how space-time was warped and shifted, will calculate the coordinates that will send me another step towards home. I rush through them, not really thinking, just transcribing from memory as quickly as possible the numbers and symbols that, after countless shifts through different permutations of my life, still burn clearly in my mind: my compass, my north star, the map charting my way home.

"Jon! You're in early today."

I turn and see Saniya, my co-director of the project, walking towards me. She is, as always, impeccably dressed, her smart outfit a stark contrast to my wrinkled clothes. I don't know why but I'm strangely relieved to see her. She's my oldest friend and the most important person on the project after me (and the one who isn't trapped in a cycle of gravitationally generated distortions of reality), so I'm probably just glad to know she'll be here to help me with the calculations.

"Did you see the news?" She holds her tablet to my face and I see the front page of the New York Times: MAYOR CALLS FOR CITY TO REFUSE REFUGEES. "I still can't believe we re-elected this asshole," she says. Her words grab onto me with their familiarity and I feel my skin prickle with déjà vu.

"I can't believe we re-elected this asshole," Saniya says, slamming her empty drink back onto the bar. "It feels like a nightmare. He's lucky we barely stumbled through Tammy in one piece. I swear, I'd almost rather the city be flooded —"

I push the fake memory away and try to focus on what Saniya is saying, but hazy images of other lives flash through my mind: water rushing down 10th Avenue; the new mayor crying in the ruins of Battery Park as she promises never again; Saniya crying and the old mayor grinning in a sun-swept Battery Park as he promises to send her people away; smoke and fire and screams and people marching and then running through the streets. It used to be easy to tell the real memories from the fake, but after so long they've started to mix and run together in my mind like paint splashed against a wall, and now it's all I can do to make out the tattered ribbons of color that are the real me. It's scary slowly losing myself like this, but if I can just get the calculations right and go home...

"Jon, are you even listening to me? Sorry, is the death of democracy boring you?"

The sarcastic edge in Saniya's voice is something I do remember and I know I'd better pay attention now. "Sorry, yeah he's terrible," I say quickly.

She gives me an odd look and I know she's surprised by my listlessness. The truth is, I've forgotten how I feel about the mayor. I mean, I know how I'm supposed to feel—the man was an anti-science crypto-racist long before the first generator test—but the emotion of it faded away a long time ago. I don't even remember if he's supposed to win his reelection or if New York is supposed to have its first woman mayor anymore. It's another reminder of how much I've lost from home.

"Can you take a look at something?" I ask, changing the subject. I run my hand across the board and bring up the first page of my equations.

Saniya gives me a lingering look before shrugging and turning to the board. As she reads, her eyes widen slightly, and after several pages she turns towards me and half-states, half-asks, "These are new solutions to the field equations?"

I nod. She means Einstein's gravitational field equations—the foundations of our quantum modeling program. They're notoriously difficult to solve and our work formulating new solutions and applications for them is one of the cornerstones of the Gravitational Field Generator Project. What I'm showing her are the results of my further work using results from the project and tests across more lives and realities than I can remember.

"You did all of this by yourself?"

"I had some inspiration and ran with it. I think we should build these into the modeling program. It'll improve our wave models of the shifts and—"

Saniya raises a hand and cuts me off. "Jon, if you think this is worth it, then I'm with you. You should have told me sooner, though. We got here as a team, remember?"

"I know, I'm sorry." I'm not, but as long as she's on board, it doesn't matter.

"Alright, walk me through this before we talk to the rest of the team." I nod and turn back to the board to walk Saniya through my equations for what feels like the thousandth time.

I hear my phone vibrate and glance at the screen: a call from Mom in California. I hesitate for a second and then silence it. There's too much work to do.

Most of the team, including Saniya, is working on building my equations into the quantum modeling program, but I'm alone in my office because I have to do this part —using the equations and data from the generator's sensor array in this shift to calculate a way home—by myself. It's much easier to explain the need to update the quantum software than the need to configure the generator to use gravity to selectively warp the fabric of space-time (sometimes I still try, but Saniya is always a pain about it). I can't finish until the rest of the team finishes its part, because until the quantum software is updated I can't analyze and determine with enough precision exactly how the gravitational fields generated in the last test distorted space-time; but fortunately, the project here is pretty advanced. We've—no, *they've*—already run a few tests of the generator and are scheduled for a full systems test next month. I'll be ready by then.

The team is excited by my new equations, of course, and some people drop by my office to talk about them. I try to be patient when they just need some clarification on the equations, but it's hard to not be curt when the conversation strays into something more theoretical. When the shifts first began what feels like a lifetime ago—in a way was many lifetimes—I was scared, confused, and even in wonder of it all; but those emotions have long since faded. I've stopped trying to understand it, stopped wondering if I'm actually traveling to new time-lines or realities or just somehow altering my own. All I really know or care about now is that after what feels like an eternity of running the generator over and over again using different coil configurations and "shifting" through an endless parade of similar but different lives, I'm finally close to getting home.

My phone vibrates again and I reach out to silence it, thinking Mom is very persistent today. As I do, I see the screen and freeze as a tingling wave washes over me. It's a message from Ely saying: "Fundraiser's going great! Guess you're not going to make it?" I instinctively start typing the reply, my fingers seeming to move on their own. I'm nearly done when I stop myself. I stare at the message I typed telling her I'll be there soon, a tingling feeling of familiarity lingering in my fingertips.

I don't know an Ely.

I can almost see her in my mind: the flash of a smile, moonlight glinting in her eyes—*she laughs warmly, her eyes sparkling and seeming to change colors*—but I push the images away and put my phone down. Memories of strangers are the most dangerous.

I turn back to the equations.

I only manage a few more hours of work before Saniya barges into my office (she never knocks) and makes me stop. Apparently, Mom asked her to make sure I was okay, which she took to mean that it was time to stop working and share a car home. I'm a little annoyed at being ordered around like a five-year old, but I'm also pretty tired and hungry, and I can't work with her harassing me like this anyway... so I agree and she calls a car for us (which I somehow end up paying for).

I'm in my kitchen a half hour later, rooting through my refrigerator for something to eat. Its contents change after each shift and I still find it vaguely interesting to wonder why. Part of it is probably from different choices I made in a particular reality—going to the Safeway around the corner rather than making the trek down to Chinatown for groceries— and part of it where in time each shift sends me, which means more or less food's been eaten relative to my "home" refrigerator. The changes are minor enough that I never experience false memories from them—no vision of me inexplicably buying that questionable-looking jar of pickles, for example (I hate pickles, so I have no idea how it got in here)—but in a way, the state of my refrigerator is a perfect microcosm of my endless shifts. Maybe, I sometimes muse, hidden somewhere in my quantum refrigerator is the key to unifying General Relativity and Quantum Mechanics and the secret to finding my way home.

After about another minute of fruitless searching I sigh. Honestly, I'd take some decent food over the secrets to physics at this point. I've just about given up and am picking up the jar of pickles when the doorbell rings. I start at the sudden sound and hit my head. Rubbing my head and cursing, I extricate myself from the refrigerator and walk to the door, wondering who it could be this late.

When I open the door, the first things I see are her eyes. They sparkle warmly in the cool light of the hallway, their color seeming to shift and change like ripples in a river. They're familiar, like I've seen them before; no, not just seen them, but *know* them. Know how they'll shimmer, how their color will flicker now from soft brown to bright green and sparkling blue.

"They're hazel," she says. "I loved them growing up. I couldn't decide which color I liked more. Whenever I had to write my eye color down, I always put brown-green-blue. I only stopped when the DMV refused to put three colors on my driver's license." She laughs and her eyes shimmer, flickering from soft brown to bright green and sparkling blue.

"Hi, sorry for coming by so late," she says.

Her eyes release me then and I see a young woman, a light coat over her cocktail dress and a large paper bag in one hand. A tingling sense of déjà vu lingers over me, and I say the thing—a feeling more than a word—still echoing in my mind: "Ely."

"Jon," she says with a smile.

"The doorman didn't tell me you were coming up," I say slowly, still feeling dazed.

"He recognized me—didn't even have to sign in. I guess I'm one step closer to completing my nefarious plan to break into your apartment and rob you." She winks and then lifts up her paper bag. "I brought you food from the fundraiser. I know how much you love free stuff."

I start to think of an excuse to send her away, remembering that every moment I'm with her I risk forgetting a little more of myself, when my stomach growls hungrily. *I do love free food,* I can't stop myself from thinking.

"Well, are you going to let me in or just stand there starving?" she asks amusedly. Her words are playful, but the blue of her eyes pierces me with their familiarity. They grab onto me and I feel them pulling me in like a river.

I should stay away. She's not real, she's dangerous...

I open my eyes and I'm sitting at my dinner table. Small boxes of food are spread out in front of me and I watch as Ely searches for plates in the kitchen. "I can't believe this is what happens when I leave you alone for a bit," she calls out. "This place is a mess!" My skin prickles and I have a feeling like I've sat here watching her open drawers and cabinets, listening to the clinking sound of plates and silverware, just like this, before. Memories bubble forward and images flash through my mind: her leaning against the kitchen counter laughing, sitting on my couch with the sun in her hair, eyes shimmering as she leans across the table towards me.

They disappear with the clink of a plate and Ely is leaning across the table, pushing a plate of large steamed buns and a pair of chopsticks towards me. "Try these," she says. "They're also vegetarian. Well, everything's vegetarian, but that's the price you pay when you put me in charge of an event."

"Chopsticks, really?" I ask, the words coming on their own. "I'm supposed to eat these with chopsticks?"

"Oh, but that's what you taught me," she replies coyly as she carefully picks up a bun with her chopsticks. "At least that's what I told the mayor. I really hope somebody got a picture of him trying." Her eyes sparkle blue with mischief as she takes a bite, and I can't help but laugh.

I stab a bun with my chopsticks and lift it to my mouth. "That's what you should have done," I say before taking a bite. The bun tastes like home, and when she bursts out laughing it makes me happy.

"So the mayor came to the fundraiser?" I ask, feeling like I already know the answer.

"Oh yes, he was shameless. Gave a big speech about always believing in the Dry Line and being there to show his continued support. After all that funding he cut…"

Her words spark something inside of me and images flash through my mind: water crashing over me as Saniya grabs onto my arm; Saniya running through a street, people and bodies and signs and smoke and chaos all around her; the world twisting and shifting through my tears as the generator's roar floods my ears. Everything's wrong and everywhere is suffering. Except home.

I need to get home.

Ely is leaning towards the flower by my window now. She gently brushes her fingers across the large round leaves and the bulb of the flower and then draws her hand away. "This is beautiful. Where did you get it?"

I look at her and remember her standing there, the sun dancing in her hair as she runs her hands across the flower, and her question feels wrong. "My mom sent it," I say hesitantly, my words also feeling off. "I don't even remember what it is, honestly."

"Is she Buddhist?"

"Yes, how did you know?" I know it doesn't make sense because I've never been here before—never known this girl before tonight—but I can't shake the feeling that this is all wrong: like I'm watching a movie that's not playing out the way it's supposed to.

"This is a lotus," she says as she traces a finger along the edge of the ceramic pot. "It's symbolic in Buddhism." I see her standing by the window with the sunlight streaming around us as she adjusts the flower pot.

"Buddhism teaches that humans are born and reborn into an endless cycle of suffering, rooted in our attachment to the illusion of the permanence of ourselves and the world around us," she says and I'm standing in front of her, her eyes pulling me in again. "A lotus grows out of the mud into a flower. When it opens, it's the promise of escape from the cycle."

The color of her eyes seem to shift and change under the dim light of my apartment, and as they pull me in, it suddenly seems like they are sparkling in sunlight. Like it's a warm summer day and the bright green leaves of Central Park are rustling behind her. "It'll be beautiful when it blooms."

The part of me that isn't me feels guilty, but after that night I tell my doorman to not let Ely up anymore and I reply to all her messages that I'm busy. The danger of fake memories alone was enough to want me to keep her away; but there was also something about that night, something about the way my skin tingled and my mind drifted—almost as if I had just run the generator and shifted—that unsettled me.

So I focus on work, and the days pass by in an indistinct blur. Mornings roll into nights into mornings again with only the familiar scrawl of the equations really standing out. I'm vaguely aware of a flurry of events unfolding outside the lab, mostly through Saniya's reports on the mayor's latest outrages: the cuts to education, the "tough on crime" initiatives in the outer boroughs, the feud with Washington over refugee resettlement. Some I half-remember from other shifts and others I'm hearing for the first time. All of them, I ignore. All I need to focus on are my equations. The world might shift and change like a storm-swept river, but the equations are my rock and as long as I hold onto them I'll find my way home.

"So there's a protest planned for the mayor's speech next week."

I look up at Saniya, her words catching my attention in a way they hadn't previously. "You're not thinking of going, are you?"

She sighs. "I know, I know. Scientists shouldn't get involved in politics, it erodes public trust in us. But how can I keep sitting here with my hands under my ass when he's attacking everything we care about?"

"Saniya, no! Please don't." The words burst out of my mouth by themselves, and even I'm surprised at the urgency in them. I don't know why, but I'm overcome by the feeling that I have to stop her.

Saniya seems taken aback as well, and looks at me quietly. "Don't worry," she says after a while. "I've got too much to do right now with your damn equations anyway."

I don't understand the sense of relief that fills me, but my skin continues tingling long after.

I'm walking with Saniya through one of the tree-lined, cobblestone paths of the "Square", the small park that connects the malls, museums, and offices that make up the Hudson Yards development. It's a clear, sunny day, but the air is crisp and cool. It's been a long time since I've walked outside like this, and it feels nice.

I stop, feeling like something is wrong. My skin is prickling, as if a cold wave had just washed over me. Saniya looks at me questioningly. "Jon?"

I look back uncertainly. What am I doing here? I feel something in my hand and look down at the paper bag I'm holding. Did we get lunch? There's so much work to do, why would I leave the lab? My mind is buzzing and it almost feels like I've shifted, but...

"Jon!" a familiar voice calls out. It's like the chime of a bell and scatters the questions roiling through my mind. I look up and see Ely ahead of us. Sunlight streams through the trees around her, and when she smiles my skin tingles and it feels like... I struggle to remember the word.

"I thought it was you," she says as she walks up.

"Ely," I say, shifting uneasily. I can feel the fake memories seeping into me, in the way her smile puts me at ease and my mind tells me she's a friend. "What are you doing here?" I ask curtly, pushing all those feelings aside.

Her eyes widen slightly and I know she's taken aback by my coldness. I fight down the feeling of guilt I tell myself isn't real. "Sorry, am I not supposed to be? We did meet here, if you remember."

She's sitting on one of the stone seating walls, the rays of sunlight streaming between the trees seeming to somehow all end with her. She laughs and tries to hold her hair away from her face as it dances in the sudden breeze.

The image fades away and I'm looking into Ely's eyes again. "I was showing some donors the riverfront," she says, breaking the silence I didn't realize had passed. "Helps to give a visual of something before you start begging people for money to fund it. Going to need a lot of that now that the mayor has officially 'completed' the public part of the Dry Line public-private partnership." She rolls her eyes but smiles, and I know she's trying to ease the tension. A part of me wants that too, but another just wants to run away.

Saniya clears her throat loudly and I realize that we've fallen into another awkward silence. "Hi, I'm Saniya," she says, shooting me an annoyed glance before stepping up and offering her hand to Ely.

"I'm Ely," Ely replies as she quickly shakes Saniya's hand. I can sense her relief at Saniya's intervention, and feel another pang of guilt. "Are you friends with Jon?"

"On the good days," Saniya says with a shrug. "Usually I just work with him."

"Oh!" Ely's eyes light up. "Jon's told me about you. You've been friends since college, right?"

Saniya raises an eyebrow and shoots me another glance. "Yes..."

"Well, Jon never told me how gorgeous you are—I love your outfit! You know, we laypeople always imagine scientists running around in white lab coats, but you're just so stylish."

Saniya's face breaks out in a grin and the tension melts away. She's a sucker for compliments. Did I tell Ely that? "Oh, this? It's nothing, I just threw it on this morning. I mean, we actually do wear lab coats at the lab..."

"I mean it. Jon, you're lucky you've had Saniya as a friend all this time. You probably wouldn't have seemed as creepy if she had been with you when we met." She gives me a quick, teasing wink.

"Ohh... I like you!" Saniya gushes. She looks at me, points at Ely a few times and stage whispers loudly, "I really like her!"

Ely laughs and takes Saniya's arm. "Come on, you're at 50 Hudson, right? I'll walk you back."

"It's okay, we can head back ourselves." Even as I say them, the words feel wrong, as if I've lived this moment before and that just wasn't what I was supposed to say.

"Oh shush, you!" Saniya snaps. "Yes Ely, you absolutely must walk us back." She pulls Ely and they start walking together towards the lab.

"It's fine," Ely says to me. "It's close, and besides, I want to hear from Saniya what you were like in college."

Saniya grins. "Oh, you would've hardly recognized him. He was this geeky little kid who didn't have a clue how to talk to real people."

Ely bursts out laughing. "Really? No way!"

"Yes! His sense of humor was the same though, his one redeeming quality..."

I feel my resistance crumbling, as if seeing them meet was the last piece of some puzzle that had been haunting me. I hesitate for a few moments as they walk ahead, and then follow. When I take the first step, it feels like a weight's been lifted; as if I've been swimming against the current of a river and finally decided to let go and drift with it.

As we walk, Ely and Saniya become engrossed in their conversation and seem to forget me. They're relaxed and comfortable, like they've known each other for years, and it feels... right. We walk past a bed of flowers and as a gust of wind picks up, I catch their fragrance in the air. It's soft and delicate, like it would disappear if I breathe too deeply; but it's so familiar, like I've smelled this exact same smell somewhere before. As I breathe in, my skin tingles and a familiar wave washes over me.

The smell comes on a cool summer breeze, soft and delicate like the flowers they come from. I smile, the fragrance lingering in my nose as I watch Ely and Saniya joking and laughing together. I'm glad they're getting along: it's important to me. The wind picks up again and the smell of the flowers drifts away with it.

The scent fades away and the memory with it. I blink a few times, feeling disoriented, like I've just woken up from a dream I'm quickly forgetting; but a part of me is telling me that there's something important about it. *Isn't this the first time they've met?*

"You know, Jon hasn't said anything about you," Saniya's voice cuts in, scattering my thoughts. "I can't believe he's been hiding you."

Ely laughs. "Well, we haven't known each other that long. What's it been Jon, a few months?"

I hesitate. "I think so..."

Ely stops and purses her lips thoughtfully. "No, longer than that I think." She looks at me, and suddenly all I see are her eyes, pulling me in as they shimmer between green and blue under the bright summer sun. "Come on, Jon, don't tell me you've forgotten already?"

I'm reviewing calculations from the sensor physics team when I suddenly think of Ely. I don't know why, but one moment

I'm cross-checking an equation and the next I remember her eyes sparkling under the sun the day she met Saniya. Didn't I realize something important that day? *When was it?*

At that moment, Saniya opens my door and walks in (she never knocks).

"Hey, what's up?" I ask.

"I missed your face. Seeing it every few hours, 12 hours a day, every day, hasn't been enough for me, so I came here to look at it again." She's impeccably dressed and looks as sharp as always. I would be hard-pressed to tell that she's been in the office every day for the past two weeks working tirelessly.

"Well, look away, take a picture. When you're done, I have work to do." I, on the other hand am particularly feeling the weight of my endless labors today, and probably look like a disheveled mess.

Saniya makes a show of looking me over and then says gravely, "On second thought, this was a bad idea: you look like crap."

I roll my eyes, but she smiles and leans against my table. "Ely and I are going to get lunch at that new Thai place at the Kitchens. Want to come?"

"You've been talking to Ely?" I'm surprised—haven't they just met?

Saniya looks at me strangely. "Um, yes? She's going to become my new best friend, if you don't get your act together. I swear, you care more about this test than me."

"That's not true." I'm doing this for her too. My memories of home are hazy and confused, but I know everything is better there for her too. I struggle to find a memory of her, and a tiny feeling of doubt begins gnawing at me.

"Jon, are you okay?" Saniya's voice cuts through my thoughts. I look up at her worried frown and realize I've been quiet for too long. "You know, you've been really... serious ever since we started working with these new equations."

"I'm fine," I say quickly. "I just want to make sure we're ready for the test." What she said is still bothering me—I know I'm doing this for her too, but I can't seem to remember why.

"Come get lunch with me and Ely."

"You go ahead, I'm in the middle of something." Was it the mayor? Maybe the mayor didn't get re-elected at home?

"Jon, the test will be fine—don't let it take over your life. That was the whole point of us agreeing to work here and building this team, remember?"

"I know, and you know I know that, but this is important. Everything will be fine after the test, I promise." Yes, that must be it. She'd be happy in a world where the mayor was somebody else.

Saniya gives me a long, doubtful look. After a while, she sighs and shrugs. "Okay, fine. I guess you were always either too smart or too lazy to really screw yourself over by overworking."

"Of course, trust me." I force a smile and my words sound more certain than I feel. *Water crashes through the doors, flooding the room, and Saniya screams.*

It's quiet as I walk through the park that runs uptown from the Square past the lab. I follow the soft yellow glow of street-lamps that seem to lead to nowhere, and as the cool night air wraps around me I'm glad I agreed to make this small escape from the lab. I can't remember the last time I've just taken a walk like this.

"Jon?" Her voice drifts to me on the back of a quiet breeze and I look up, not sure if I heard a memory or something

real. *I see her walking towards me then, hair rustling quietly in the wind. The moonlight seems to guide her way, and gives her eyes a faint brown-green sparkle. I have a feeling like I'm seeing something from a dream.*

"It is you," Ely says as she steps in front of me. "What are you doing out here?"

"I was… going for a walk," I say slowly, feeling like I've just woken up from a dream—or a memory.

"This late? Did you come from the lab?"

I nod. "I was working and…" Why did I come here? Images flash through my mind. "My mom…" I trail off uncertainly.

"She what? Sent you to your room for being bad?" Ely says with a slight smile.

I relax. That's right actually. Mom had been talking to Saniya again and sent me a flood of messages telling me to stop working so hard before I had a heart attack like Dad. I don't know why I forgot that for a moment, but Ely reminding me is reassuring. I begin lowering the guard I didn't realize I had put up. "Something like that," I say. "She told me to go for a walk first and get connected to nature."

"She sounds great. We'd probably get along—you know me and nature."

I'm not sure I do but nod anyway. "Well, I guess this is about as close to nature as you get in Manhattan," I say as I look around for what feels like the first time. The park feels smaller now and I'm conscious of the buildings rising up around us.

Ely's eyes light up. "Hey, you want to see something amazing?"

I hesitate, but before I can reply she grabs my hand and pulls me with her. "Come on, it's not far. I promise it's worth it."

Her hand feels soft and warm in mine and I instinctively squeeze it to keep it from slipping away. My eyes trace the line of my hand into hers and along her arm to the curve of her shoulder. Moonlight streams down around her and seems to light a path ahead of us. She looks back at me, her eyes a deep ocean blue, and smiles and squeezes my hand back.

She leads us out of the park and we walk quickly through the near-empty streets of West Side Manhattan, talking about nothing and everything: fleeting words quickly forgotten that put me more at ease than I've felt in a long time. We reach the West Side Highway and run across the empty road like kids, her laughter lingering in the night air. She holds my hand the entire way and as I watch the curve of her shoulders rise and fall and the moonlight dance in her hair, my skin tingles and I feel like I'm being pulled into a dream, or perhaps the memory of one.

On the other side of the highway we reach a long metal fence and Ely finally lets go. My empty hand feels cold, and I clench it as I watch her type into a keypad and open a door in the fence. She takes us through into a long park that stretches along the Hudson. I follow her over the grass past scattered trees and up a gentle slope. We sit down at the top and I look down another slope at the Hudson, bathed in moonlight.

"Welcome to the Dry Line," Ely says with a sweeping flourish of her hand. "I can't believe we've known each other this long and I haven't taken you before."

I shift at the reminder that she doesn't really belong in my life, but look around. In a way, the success or failure of the Dry Line determines whether I'm home, but I've never paid it much attention. I see that there's still a lot of work being done: piles of dirt, construction equipment, half-assembled structures, and unplanted trees cover the area. "Where are the flood barriers?" I ask.

"You're sitting on them. The idea was to build something natural that blends into the environment, so you wouldn't notice even if you're right on top of it."

"Like me just now?"

"Exactly." She flashes a satisfied smile. "There are metal locks on the East Side under the FDR, but here we were able to get along with nature a little more. Pretty awesome, right?"

I look down the slope of what I now realize is a long series of hills running along the length of the Hudson. Under the dim glow of the moon, the quietly rustling grass shifts seamlessly into the softly rippling waters of the river. "Yes, it is," I say.

"You know, it barely survived the storm. It wasn't nearly this complete then. So much water got through..." she trails off quietly.

Images flash through my mind: water swallowing up people and bodies floating quietly down flooded avenues. "How bad would it have been?"

"It's hard to say, there are so many variables. The storm weakening, the funding you helped us get... Honestly, I try not to think of it."

I helped her? I'm both surprised and not, and ignore both feelings. "Not at all?" I ask instead.

She laughs softly. "You're just like Saniya—she loves talking about this. She says it's our fault the mayor was re-elected, because he got all the credit for saving the city."

"Maybe it would've been okay." I think of home again. I've taken for granted for so long that everything's better there, but I can't really remember why. It's like an old equation I've forgotten the steps to solving and now all I have is the answer: go home. "Maybe the damage wouldn't have been too bad, and the mayor wouldn't have been re-elected and..." I stop as I realize how obsessive I must sound.

Ely regards me thoughtfully though. After several long moments, she asks, "Have you ever been to a forest, Jon?"

"Does Central Park count?" I feel like I want to see her smile again and somehow know she'll like this joke.

She rolls her eyes but smiles slightly and I relax. "You're such a city boy—I'll have to take you to a real forest sometime.

The Catskills are nice. We should go there, if you really want to get connected to nature."

My skin tingles but no images flash through my mind. It's just a feeling like I've lived this moment before.

"Sometimes when I'm there I just sit and listen to the wind and the birds, and it feels like... everything is connected. Like even though I'm trying to stay still, the world keeps moving and I'm not supposed to fight it." She looks at me and her eyes glimmer a deep brown under the pale moonlight. "Nothing is permanent, Jon. Not what's happening now and certainly not what might have been. The world is always moving. The only way we can really stay still is to live in each moment and move with it."

She turns back towards the river and looks into it quietly. I follow her gaze and begin to barely make out the ripples of the waters' ebbs and flows under the dim glow of the moon. I think I can almost see myself in them.

As I get closer to completing the calculations, the days begin to feel strangely disjointed. I don't know why, but each one feels somehow disconnected from the next, as if every morning I'm stepping from one life into another. It's a feeling that possesses me more and more every day: a hazy, lingering, uncertainty that leaves my skin tingling. I know I have a word for it, but it keeps slipping my mind. The only things that feel clear are my equations, and I throw myself into them, taking comfort in their familiarity. I'm being tossed around in a constantly shifting river, the currents pulling me under, and they're my rock. One day I begin to lose even that.

"This isn't right!" I shout again, slamming my hands on the table in frustration.

The team leaders around me in the main lab flinch. They're not used to seeing me like this, and are uncomfortable, but I don't care. I just glare at the rows of equations and calculations on the digital board that I *know* are wrong.

Saniya also doesn't care. She spins me around by my shoulder and pins me with a cold stare. "Dammit, Jon, get a grip of yourself. We've been going over this all day. They're *right* and they're based on *your* equations."

I understand logically what she's saying. The math makes sense and we went through the work logs all the way back to the beginning to make sure. But I also know, as surely as I know my name, that it can't be right—the team *must* have messed up somewhere—because when I combine our work to calculate the coil configuration for the next test, I get the exact same one I used for my last shift. It was, in effect, telling me I'm already home.

"Jon," Saniya says, more gently this time. "Are you alright?"

"It doesn't make sense..." I sigh. If it was just close, maybe I could explain it, but the exact same configuration? It's impossible...

"Alright, everybody take the rest of the day off!" Saniya says suddenly. An uneasy murmur starts that she quickly cuts off. "You heard me! Life is short, get out of here and do something meaningful with it."

The others clear the lab quietly after that, though I catch a few sidelong glances. Saniya waits until they're all gone, and then looks at me worriedly. "Seriously Jon, what's going on? You know the calculations are right. Since when did you start trusting your math over mine, anyway?"

I look back at the board. She's right, and yet… "I'm sorry Saniya, just… give me some time." To convince myself that I'm wrong and not the world? It goes against everything I've learned from countless shifts.

"Why don't you take the day off too? Give Ely a call, take her to dinner."

"Ely? Why?" I don't even remember the last time I saw her, much less how she could help.

"Don't be an asshole to her too, okay? At least I know when you're not being yourself." Saniya gives me a look like she's scolding a child. "Anyway, if you're really going to spend all day confirming my work's better than yours, then I'm going to go see the mayor's speech with some non-crazy friends."

I feel a surge of fear. "You're going to a protest?"

"Protest? Why would I protest New York's first female mayor? We're going to celebrate!"

I stare at where Saniya had been for a while after she leaves. What she said feels wrong too, but for the life of me I can't remember why.

The elevator doors open and I step wearily out into the lobby. I worked all afternoon and feel more tired and less sure of myself than when I started. Saniya was right—everything made sense: her math, the equations, everything—and I still know that isn't possible. I hesitate as a thought I've been avoiding sneaks up on me again: *Could I be remembering something wrong?*

A loud alarm screeches from my phone and I pull it out of my pocket in annoyance. As I look at the message on the screen, my skin tingles with electricity and a familiar wave pulls me in.

I read the message on my phone: "EMERGENCY ALERT. Mandatory evacuation in effect in Manhattan. Go to nearest evacuation point immediately."

I hear a loud splash and look up to see Saniya stumble out of the emergency stairwell into the knee-deep water that's flooded the lobby. I'm so relieved to see her that I forget for a moment the storm raging just outside. "Saniya!" I shout.

She looks at me in surprise. "Jon? What the hell are you doing here?"

"Looking for you, you idiot! What are you still doing here—we have to get out of the city now!"

I step forward and my feet sinks into the cold water with a splash. I look around the suddenly dark and empty lobby in confusion; outside I hear the angry howling of a storm. I look down at the phone still in my hand and read the message: "EMERGENCY ALERT. FLOODING IMMINENT. SEEK HIGH GROUND IMMEDIATELY."

Where am I? Wasn't I just in the elevator?

"Jon!" Someone grabs me by my shoulder and I turn to see Saniya. "You saw the message, get back upstairs!" She pushes me towards the stairwell and starts wading through the water towards the entrance.

"Where are you going?" I shout after her.

"To get my grandmother! She lives in a walk-up and still writes me letters!"

I wrap one arm around the pole as the water crashes angrily over us. My other hand clings desperately to Saniya's, trying to pull her closer to me even as the water tears us apart. I want to look back at her, to find her face and tell her to hold on, but the water blinds me and I feel her fingers slowly slip out of mine. "Jon!" she shouts, though I barely hear her over the storm and water. "Just let—"

"Saniya, no!" I start to rush after her, and am blinded by smoke. I fall to my knees on what feels like rough asphalt, coughing and suddenly aware of the screaming and shouting surrounding me. Shadowy figures, half-hidden in the smoke, run all around me. Shots ring out and I hear sirens echoing in the distance. My skin is tingling and my mind feels heavy, almost as if I had just shifted.

"Jon..." a voice rasps out. I feel a hand brush weakly against mine and instinctively take it. *This... this is...* The smoke clears slightly, and I see Saniya lying on the ground, a jagged flower of blood blooming across her chest.

"Saniya, no, no..." I mutter, a numbing fear rising up inside me. This happened before... It doesn't make sense, but some part of me is telling me that this happened before and I'll make it okay, I'll fix it and we'll go home. "I'll fix it, don't worry I'll fix it. It's all in the equations. I'll fix it and we're going to go home..." I repeat the words desperately. I don't know what they mean, only that they have to be right.

Saniya smiles faintly up at me. "It's okay, Jon..." she murmurs. "It's okay... just let go..." I can't see her anymore through the smoke and the tears stinging my eyes, and the generator's roar floods my ears.

I open my eyes, feeling confused and disoriented. What am I doing? There's something I'm supposed to do... "My name is Jon, I'm a physicist," I say, becoming aware now that I'm sitting by a table. The words are familiar and comforting, and I cling onto them as I try to shake off the disorientation that always comes after a test.

No, that's not right... "My name is Jon," I say again. There hasn't been a test yet. I've... what have I been doing? "My name is Jon, I'm—"

"Did you forget your name, Jonathan S. Lee?"

The voice—light, playful, and *familiar*—cuts through my daze and I turn towards it. I see Ely leaning towards a window. Sunlight streams through it, falling all around her, bathing my apartment with a soft, white glow.

Jonathan. That's right. I can't remember the last time somebody called me that, but that's me and I'm with Ely in my apartment. I'm sitting by my dinner table, and there's an open jar of pickles near my hand. Everything seems to be in its place, and Mom's Buddha statue contemplates me nearby. Slowly, the fog around my mind begins to drift away.

Ely is adjusting a white ceramic bowl by the window. Long green stems shoot up out of it, most of them ending in large roundish leaves; the tallest stem though thrusts above the leaves and ends in the slender red bulb of a flower. After a few moments, Ely stops and nods. She turns to look at me, her eyes shimmering green in the sunlight and the bright green leaves of Central Park rustling behind her.

"It's a lotus flower," she says. "It should bloom by the end of summer if you manage not to kill it first. I think even you'll be okay with this one though—it's super easy to take care of. You just need to keep the water level right, and then just let it grow." She gently brushes her fingers across the large round leaves and the bulb of the flower before drawing her hand away.

"You got this for me?" I ask. The question feels important.

"Well, it was your mom's idea, but I'll take some credit too. She ordered me around and I listened to her." She laughs softly and walks over to me. As she looks at me her eyes draw me in with the way they seem to shimmer and shift between all their colors. "I think it's going to bloom soon," she says as she sits down and takes my hands in hers. They're warm and familiar and I squeeze them instinctively. "It'll be beautiful when it does."

Her words are the first things that feel right to me in a long time.

I'm staring through the reinforced glass windows at the end of the generator control room. A steady electric hum emanates from the chamber on the other side and I watch as the eight cavorite columns inside shift and rotate into the positions I calculated: the configuration that would...

I blink a few times, feeling disoriented. I look around and see Saniya next to me in front of the main control panel and the rest of the team positioned at the various monitoring stations. *What am I doing here?*

"Test configuration set," Saniya says as the coils lock into place with loud, hissing snaps. She shakes her head. "You're going to have to explain to me again later why we're using this completely random configuration for our first test."

That's right, I finally figured out what was wrong with the calculations... right?

"Beginning warm-up cycle," Saniya says. She taps on the screen of her panel and the coils inside the chamber light up and the electric hum grows louder.

I can't help but feel like I'm missing something, but I'm not sure what. The flashes have cone more frequently lately: real and fake memories swirling confusingly together, so vivid they often seem to spill into reality. They make sense and they don't and sometimes I wonder if they ever really ended or if I'm still stumbling through a memory now... This should terrify me, but...

Nothing is permanent, Jon. Not what's happening now and certainly not what might have been.

Who had said that? Somebody I knew? Somebody important to me...

A loud beep scatters my thoughts and I see the chamber again. "Warm-up cycle complete," Saniya announces. "All stations confirm systems green." She turns and looks at me expectantly. "Are you ready, Jon?"

I hesitate, not sure what I'm supposed to do. After a few moments, I nod. "Start the generator."

Home. I'm supposed to go home.

"Activating the generator," Saniya says as she taps her screen. The hum of electricity grows louder as power courses through the coils. The laser sensor array blankets the generator chamber in angry red beams and a murmur of excitement ripples through the team.

Not much longer now. My thoughts are still scattered, and I press my hands against the cold metal of the control panel, focusing on how it feels.

Her hand feels soft and warm in mine and I instinctively squeeze it to keep it from slipping away. My eyes follow the line of my hand into hers and along her arm to the curve of her shoulder. Sunlight dances in her hair and I breathe in the fresh scent of pine and early morning dew. Rays of sunlight burst between the leaves of the trees, piercing the forest canopy with lances of light, and seeming to light a path ahead of us. She looks back at me, her eyes a brilliant sky blue, and smiles and squeezes my hand back.

The electric hum of the coils is louder now. I reach for her hand and feel only cold metal. Everything seems distant and I'm not sure where I am, but the scent of pine lingers in the air. A forest... didn't she say she'd take me to one? But she didn't—not yet. None of this makes sense...

"Huh, I just had the weirdest feeling..." Saniya says, and her voice draws me back to the room, to the generator. Yes, the generator, that's where I am.

"What... did you say?" I stammer, feeling like I've just woken up.

"I just had a feeling like we've done this before. Like I was standing right here with you watching this happen before. It feels like..."

Déjà vu. That was the word. That was the word I'd forgotten.

The room seems to spin around me and a thousand images from a thousand lives flash before me. Saniya: lying in the street, dying in the street; slipping into the water, pulling me from it; laying her grandmother down; sobbing at Battery

Park, tears of joy running down her cheeks. Ely: a park, a forest, a roof, my room, my arms around her, her arms around me, and her eyes—always shifting, never changing: her eyes. And me: in the lab, in my apartment, the city flooding outside and covered in smoke and fire, pouring over the equations—always shifting, never changing: the equations.

I see them as they really are: memories of pasts yet to be, futures already come, and everything in between—all connected. I'm sitting with Ely on the unfinished banks of a river and see my life and all those moments rushing by in the water: ebbs and flows, ripples and whirls that split and mingle and change each other, moving forwards and backwards all at once before finally joining together again.

The world is always moving. The only way we can really stay still is to live in each moment and move with it. All this time I thought the generator—*I thought I—* was the only one shifting the world; but I finally realize now what all the flashes and disjointed memories I've been experiencing mean. Perhaps it was the generator and the endless shifts it sent me through that allowed me to finally see it, but the world is always shifting and changing too, and when it does... if it touches you, it feels like déjà vu.

I see the generator now, hear its electric hum echoing loudly through the room. I know where I am and what to do: I have to escape the cycle. I have to stop fighting and surrender myself to the river. I have to accept where the world wants me to go.

"Saniya, stop the test."

"What did you say?"

"Stop the test!"

"Are you crazy?! Why?" she looks at me eyes wide in disbelief.

"Saniya please just trust me, we have to stop the test now!" I summon every bit of pleading, urgency, desperation, sincerity, and truth I can muster—across a thousand lifetimes of friendship—as I look into her eyes.

She hesitates for only a few moments longer before turning to the control panel. "God damn men..." she says loudly as she taps the screen. Minutes pass and her tapping continues, becoming gradually more urgent; but the hum of the generator seems to only get louder. Finally, she stops and looks up, a panicked look on her face. "It's not stopping!"

"What do you mean? Did you manually cut the power?"

"Of course I did! But the coils are still active! Gravitational distortions are getting stronger!" Saniya begins shouting orders at the team and I feel fear rippling through the room. The humming of the coils turns into a roar, and I can barely hear myself think. As the sound grows even louder, I see the red beams of the sensor array begin to distort, slowly twisting like they're caught in a whirlpool.

"Jon! Do you see this?" Saniya exclaims.

The sound of the generator becomes thunderous and everything around me begins to twist and warp. I begin to feel like all I'm really seeing is a faint impression of some forgotten memory. The coils, the chamber, my hands on the panel—they all seem so indistinct, like they aren't really there.

A hand grabs onto mine and I turn to see Saniya, eyes wide and fear etched across her slowly twisting face. I remember her lying on the street, blood spreading across her chest like a red flower and fear rising in mine.

"It's okay, Saniya." I squeeze her hand back. "It's okay, just let—"

I feel then like *I'm* twisting, my body being pulled in all directions and back again at once. And then the noise is gone and everything is dark. I can't feel Saniya's hand or my own and the only thing I hear is the echo of a familiar voice, telling me things I wanted to say.

I walk through the Square, hugging the large brown take-out bag in my arms. I asked Saniya to get lunch with me, but she's been wanting to spend most of her time in the lab lately; so I offered to pick something up for her, which quickly escalated into buying burritos for the rest of the team. Ah, the duties of a co-director...

Well, if that means Saniya's stuck in the lab checking my calculations while I enjoy this lovely summer day, who am I to complain?

Something catches my eyes and I stop. I'm not sure what it is but I turn and look to my side. I see her then, sitting on one of the stone seating walls, the rays of sunlight streaming between the trees seeming to somehow all end with her.

She's reading a book, and something draws me to her. I'm not the type of person to approach strangers in a park (that's more Saniya's thing) but I lower my bag of burritos and walk up to her. "Hello," I try.

She looks up at me and I'm struck by the way her eyes seem to shimmer and shift colors as she moves. "Hi," she says, giving me a not-unfriendly smile.

I hesitate, not sure what I'm doing or what to say, when it suddenly comes to me. "Do you work at the Dry Line?"

She glances down at the folders by her side, held down against the wind by a small jar of pickles and marked in large block letters: DRY LINE WEST SIDE COASTAL RESILIENCY PROJECT. "How did you guess that?" she asks, her lips quirking slightly.

I shift uncomfortably. "Ah, I mean..." This is not going how I expected. What had I expected? "Do you need help with it?" I blurt out.

She purses her lips and gives me a curious look. "You know, that actually might be one of the better pick-up lines I've heard. Not that that's saying much— they're all pretty bad."

I feel my face heating up. "That's not what I'm doing! It's a really important project and I want to help..."

She laughs and lifts a hand up to hold her hair away from her face as it dances in a sudden gust of wind. "I'm sorry," she says, seeming embarrassed herself now. "That's really nice of you."

"I really do want to help," I say again lamely.

Her face becomes thoughtful and she regards me quietly. As she looks at me, her eyes draw me in. They sparkle warmly in the light of the summer sun, their color seeming to shift and change like ripples in a river. They're so familiar, like I've seen them before; no, not just seen them, but *know* them. Know how they'll shimmer, how their color will flicker now from soft brown to bright green and sparkling blue.

"Sorry," she says after what feels like a long time. "I just had the strangest feeling that we've met before."

I continue looking at her quietly for a few moments more and then hold out my hand. "I'm Jonathan."

She puts her book down and shakes my hand. There's something warm and familiar about her touch.

"I'm Elysia," she says. "But my friends call me Ely."

"Elysia?" I feel like I've just remembered something I'd forgotten.

"It means home." She smiles and her eyes seem to settle onto a light blue that reflects the sky. I see myself in them.

If you liked Phong Quan's story "It Feels Like Déjà Vu", leave a comment online at Metaphorosis. Authors love that!

About the story

"It Feels Like Déjà Vu" is the culmination of many different influences from throughout my life. I wrote the first scene many years ago while I was in college, involving the two (at that time unnamed) main characters talking as a shift occurred. In that scene, the character that would become Ely is trying to remind Jon of their relationship and he is trying to shut her out just as a shift happens and she disappears. Nothing else came of that, though the scene and premise of "shifts" stuck in my head. Many years later, when I was working in New York and having my soul crushed in corporate law, I decided to start writing again to preserve my sanity and chose to create a story from that basic premise. The setting became New York, a city I loved, and I decided to use the "shifts" as a way to explore the Buddhist concepts of impermanence and the karmic cycles--something my parents believed in and talked about a lot. Finally, Ely's character and personality are based on the person I was dating at the time, and the focus in the story on environmental issues and nature are a reflection of her passion for them. Those three basic building blocks are the foundation of the story that I ultimately wrote and you can read on *Metaphorosis* now.

A question for the author

Q: If you could have any super power, what would it be?

A: My superpower would almost certainly be the ability to stop or slow time--there just isn't enough time in the world for me to do everything I want to do.

About the author

Phong's parents are from tropical Vietnam, so after they immigrated to the United States of course he was born in Minnesota on April 1st on the last day of a big snow storm—a great April Fool's joke for everyone involved. Immediately afterwards, his family moved to sunny California where he was raised. Phong eventually became a corporate lawyer, working in New York, Beijing and now Singapore, where he is currently based.

Copyright

Metaphorosis Publishing

Metaphorosis offers beautifully written science fiction and fantasy. Our projects include:

Metaphorosis Magazine

Metaphorosis, a weekly magazine of SFF short stories, including stories from all the authors in this anthology. Find out more at magazine.metaphorosis.com, and sign up to be notified of new stories.

Metaphorosis Books

Recent books from Metaphorosis can be found at books.metaphorosis.com, and include:

Metaphorosis 2017   **Metaphorosis 2016**

All the stories from *Metaphorosis* magazine's second year.

Almost all the stories from *Metaphorosis* magazine's first year.

Metaphorosis: Best of 2017

The best science fiction and fantasy stories from *Metaphorosis'* 2nd year.

Metaphorosis: Best of 2016

The best science fiction and fantasy stories from *Metaphorosis'* 1st year.

Reading 5X5

Reading 5X5

Five stories, five times

Writers' Edition

Twenty-five SFF authors, five base stories, five versions of each – see how different writers take on the same material.

All the stories from the regular, readers' edition, plus two extra stories, the story seed, and authors' notes.

Best Vegan SFF of 2017

The best vegan science fiction and fantasy stories of 2017!

Best Vegan SFF of 2016

The best vegan science fiction and fantasy stories of 2016!

Susurrus

A darkly romantic story of magic, love, and suffering.